THE NECKLACE OF
Princess Fiorimonde
AND OTHER STORIES
Mary de Morgan

Illustrated by Sylvie Monti

HUTCHINSON
London   Sydney   Auckland   Johannesburg

All rights reserved
First published in 1990
by Hutchinson Children's Books
an imprint of Random Century Group Ltd
20 Vauxhall Bridge Road, London SW1V 2SA

Random Century Australia Pty Ltd
20 Alfred Street, Sydney, NSW 2061

Random Century New Zealand Ltd
PO Box 40-086, Glenfield, Auckland 10, New Zealand

Random Century South Africa (Pty) Ltd
PO Box 337, Bergvlei, 2012, South Africa

Designed by Paul Welti
Printed and bound in Great Britain by
Butler & Tanner Ltd, Frome and London

British Library Cataloguing in Publication Data

De Morgan, Mary
    The necklace of Princess Fiorimonde
    I. Title II. Monti, Sylvie
    823.8 [J]

ISBN 0-09-174077-0

CONTENTS

One

THE NECKLACE
OF PRINCESS
FIORIMONDE

ONCE THERE LIVED A KING, WHOSE WIFE WAS DEAD, BUT WHO had a most beautiful daughter – so beautiful that everyone thought she must be good as well, instead of which the Princess was really very wicked, and practised witchcraft and black magic which she had learned from an old witch who lived in a hut on the side of a lonely mountain. This old witch was wicked and hideous, and no one but the King's daughter knew that she lived there; but at night, when everyone else was asleep, the Princess, whose name was Fiorimonde, used to visit her by stealth to learn sorcery. It was only the witch's arts which had made Fiorimonde so beautiful that there was no one like her in the world, and in return the Princess helped her with all her tricks, and never told anyone she was there.

The time came when the King began to think he should like his daughter to marry, so he summoned his council and said, 'We have no son to reign after our death, so we had best seek for a suitable prince to marry to our royal daughter and then, when we are too old, he shall be king in our stead.' And all the council said he was very wise, and it would be well for the Princess to marry. So heralds were sent to all neighbouring kings and princes to say that the King would choose a husband for the Princess, who should be king after him. But when

Fiorimonde heard this she wept with rage, for she knew quite well that if she had a husband he would find out how she went to visit the old witch, and would stop her practising magic, and then she would lose her beauty.

When night came, and everyone in the palace was fast asleep, the Princess went to her bedroom window and softly opened it. Then she took from her pocket a handful of peas and held them out of the window and chirruped low, and there flew down from the roof a small brown bird and sat upon her wrist and began to eat the peas. No sooner had it swallowed them than it began to grow and grow and grow till it was so big that the Princess could not hold it, but let it stand on the windowsill, and still it grew and grew and grew till it was as large as an ostrich. Then the Princess climbed out of the window and seated herself on the bird's back, and at once it flew straight away over the tops of the trees till it came to the mountain where the old witch dwelt, and stopped in front of the door of her hut.

The Princess jumped off, and muttered some words through the keyhole, when a croaking voice from within called,

'Why do you come tonight? Have I not told you I wished to be left alone for thirteen nights; why do you disturb me?'

'But I beg of you to let me in,' said the Princess, 'for I am in trouble and want your help.'

'Come in then,' said the voice; and the door flew open, and the Princess trod into the hut, in the middle of which, wrapped in a grey cloak which almost hid her, sat the witch. Princess Fiorimonde sat down near her, and told her her story. How the King wished her to

marry, and had sent word to the neighbouring princes, that they might make offers for her.

'This is truly bad hearing,' croaked the old witch, 'but we shall beat them yet; and you must deal with each Prince as he comes. Would you like them to become dogs, to come at your call, or birds, to fly in the air, and sing of your beauty, or will you make them all into beads, the beads of such a necklace as never woman wore before, so that they may rest upon your neck, and you may take them with you always?'

'The necklace! the necklace!' cried the Princess, clapping her hands with joy. 'That will be best of all, to sling them upon a string and wear them around my throat. Little will the courtiers know whence come my new jewels.'

'But this is a dangerous play,' quoth the witch, 'for, unless you are very careful, you yourself may become a bead and hang upon the string with the others, and there you will remain till someone cuts the string, and draws you off.'

'Nay, never fear,' said the Princess, 'I will be careful, only tell me what to do, and I will have great princes and kings to adorn me, and all their greatness shall not help them.'

Then the witch dipped her hand into a black bag which stood on the ground beside her, and drew out a long gold thread.

The ends were joined together, but no one could see the joins, and however much you pulled, it would not break. It would easily go over Fiorimonde's head, and the witch slipped it on her neck saying,

'Now mind, while this hangs here you are safe enough, but if once you join your fingers around the string you too will meet the fate of

your lovers, and hang upon it yourself. As for the kings and princes who would marry you, all you have to do is to make them close their fingers around the chain, and at once they will be strung upon it as bright hard beads, and there they shall remain, till it is cut and they drop off.'

'This is really delightful,' cried the Princess; 'and I am already quite impatient for the first to come that I may try.'

'And now,' said the witch, 'since you are here, and there is yet time, we will have a dance, and I will summon the guests.' So saying, she took from a corner a drum and pair of drumsticks, and going to the door, began to beat upon it. It made a terrible rattling. In a moment came flying through the air all sorts of forms. There were little dark elves with long tails, and goblins who chattered and laughed, and other witches who rode on broomsticks. There was one wicked fairy in the form of a large cat, with bright green eyes, and another came sliding in like a long shining viper.

Then, when all had arrived, the witch stopped drumming, and, going to the middle of the hut, stamped on the floor, and a trap door opened in the ground. The old witch stepped through it, and led the way down a narrow dark passage, to a large underground chamber, and all her strange guests followed, and here they all danced and made merry in a terrible way, but at first sound of cockcrow all the guests disappeared with a whiff, and the Princess hastened up the dark passage again, and out of the hut to where her big bird still waited for her, and mounting its back she flew home in a trice. Then, when she had stepped in at her bedroom window, she poured into a cup, from a small black bottle, a few drops of magic water, and gave it to the bird to drink, and as it sipped it grew smaller, and smaller, till at last it had quite regained its natural size, and hopped on to the roof as before, and the

Princess shut her window, and got into bed, and fell asleep, and no one knew of her strange journey, or where she had been.

Next day Fiorimonde declared to her father the King, that she was quite willing to wed any prince he should fix upon as a husband for her, at which he was much pleased, and soon after informed her, that a young king was coming from over the sea to be her husband. He was king of a large rich country, and would take back his bride with him to his home. He was called King Pierrot. Great preparations were made for his arrival, and the Princess was decked in her finest array to greet him, and when he came all the courtiers said, 'This is truly a proper husband for our beautiful Princess,' for he was strong and handsome, with black hair, and eyes like sloes. King Pierrot was delighted with Fiorimonde's beauty, and was happy as the day is long; and all things went merrily till the evening before the marriage. A great feast was held, at which the Princess looked lovelier than ever dressed in a red gown, the colour of the inside of a rose, but she wore no jewels nor ornaments of any kind, save one shining gold string round her milk-white throat.

When the feast was done, the Princess stepped from her golden chair at her father's side, and walked softly into the garden, and stood under an elm tree looking at the shining moon. In a few moments King Pierrot followed her, and stood beside her, looking at her and wondering at her beauty.

'Tomorrow, then, my sweet Princess, you will be my Queen, and share all I possess. What gift would you wish me to give you on our wedding day?'

'I would have a necklace wrought of the finest gold and jewels to be found, and just the length of this gold cord which I wear around my throat,' answered Princess Fiorimonde.

'Why do you wear that cord?' asked King Pierrot; 'it has no jewel nor ornament about it.'

'Nay, but there is no cord like mine in all the world,' cried Fiorimonde, and her eyes sparkled wickedly as she spoke; 'it is as light as a feather, but stronger than an iron chain. Take it in both hands and try to break it, that you may see how strong it is'; and King Pierrot took the cord in both hands to pull it hard; but no sooner were his fingers closed around it than he vanished like a puff of smoke, and on the cord appeared a bright, beautiful bead – so bright and beautiful as was never bead before – clear as crystal, but shining with all colours – green, blue, and gold.

Princess Fiorimonde gazed down at it and laughed aloud.

'Aha, my proud lover! Are you there?' she cried with wicked glee; 'my necklace bids fair to beat all others in the world,' and she caressed the bead with the tips of her soft, white fingers, but was careful that they did not close round the string. Then she returned into the banqueting hall, and spoke to the King.

'Pray, sire,' said she, 'send someone at once to find King Pierrot, for, as he was talking to me a minute ago, he suddenly left me, and I am afraid lest I may have given him offence, or perhaps he is ill.'

The King desired that the servants should seek for King Pierrot all over the grounds, and seek him they did, but nowhere was he to be found, and the old King looked offended.

'Doubtless he will be ready tomorrow in time for the wedding,' quoth he, 'but we are not best pleased that he should treat us in this way.'

Princess Fiorimonde had a little maid called Yolande. She was a bright-faced girl with merry brown eyes, but she was not beautiful like Fiorimonde, and she did not love her mistress, for she was afraid of her, and suspected her of her wicked ways. When she undressed her that night she noticed the gold cord, and the one bright bead upon it, and as she combed the Princess's hair she looked over her shoulder into the looking glass, and saw how she laughed, and how fondly she looked at the cord, and caressed the bead, again and again with her fingers.

'That is a wonderful bead on your Highness's cord,' said Yolande, looking at its reflection in the mirror; 'surely it must be a bridal gift from King Pierrot.'

'And so it is, little Yolande,' cried Fiorimonde, laughing merrily; 'and the best gift he could give me. But I think one bead alone looks ugly and ungainly; soon I hope I shall have another, and another, and another, all as beautiful as the first.'

Then Yolande shook her head, and said to herself, 'This bodes no good.'

Next morning all was prepared for the marriage, and the Princess was dressed in white satin and pearls with a long white lace veil over her, and a bridal wreath on her head, and she stood waiting among her grandly dressed ladies, who all said that such a beautiful bride had never been seen in the world before. But just as they were preparing to go down to the fine company in the hall, a messenger came in great haste summoning the Princess at once to her father the King, as he was much perplexed.

'My daughter,' cried he, as Fiorimonde in all her bridal array entered the room where he sat alone, 'what can we do? King Pierrot is nowhere to be found; I fear lest he may have been seized by robbers and basely murdered for his rich clothes, or carried away to some mountain and left there to starve. My soldiers are gone far and wide to seek him – and we shall hear of him ere day is done – but where there is no bridegroom there can be no bridal.'

'Then let it be put off, my father,' cried the Princess, 'and tomorrow we shall know if it is for a wedding, or a funeral, we must dress'; and she pretended to weep, but even then could hardly keep from laughing.

So the wedding guests went away, and the Princess laid aside her bridal dress, and all waited anxiously for news of King Pierrot; and no news came. So at last everyone gave him up for dead, and mourned for him, and wondered how he had met his fate.

Princess Fiorimonde put on a black gown, and begged to be allowed to live in seclusion for one month in which to grieve for King Pierrot; but when she was again alone in her bedroom she sat before her looking-glass and laughed till tears ran down her cheeks; and Yolande watched her, and trembled, when she heard her laughter. She noticed, too, that beneath her black gown, the Princess still wore her gold cord, and did not move it night or day.

The month had barely passed away when the King came to his daughter, and announced that another suitor had presented himself, whom he should much like to be her husband. The Princess agreed quite obediently to all her father said; and it was arranged that the marriage should take place. This new prince was called Prince Hildebrandt. He came from a country far north, of which one day he would be king. He was tall, and fair, and strong, with flaxen hair and bright blue eyes. When Princess Fiorimonde saw his portrait she was much pleased, and said, 'By all means let him come, and the sooner the better.' So she put off her black clothes, and again great preparations were made for a wedding; and King Pierrot was quite forgotten.

Prince Hildebrandt came, and with him many fine gentlemen, and they brought beautiful gifts for the bride. The evening of his arrival all went well, and again there was a grand feast, and Fiorimonde looked so beautiful that Prince Hildebrandt was delighted; and this time she did not leave her father's side, but sat by him all the evening.

Early next morning at sunrise, when everyone was still sleeping, the Princess rose, and dressed herself in a plain white gown, and brushed all her hair over her shoulders, and crept quietly downstairs into the palace gardens; then she walked on till she came beneath the window of Prince Hildebrandt's room, and here she paused and began to sing a little song as sweet and joyous as a lark's. When Prince Hildebrandt heard it he got up and went to the window and looked out to see who sang, and when he saw Fiorimonde standing in the red sunrise-light, which made her hair look gold and her face rosy, he made haste to dress himself and go down to meet her.

'My Princess,' cried he, as he stepped into the garden beside her. 'This is indeed great happiness to meet you here so early. Tell me why do you come out at sunrise to sing by yourself?'

'I come that I may see the colours of the sky – red, blue, and gold,' answered the Princess. 'Look, there are no such colours to be seen anywhere, unless, indeed, it be in this bead which I wear here on my golden cord.'

'What is that bead, and where did it come from?' asked Hildebrandt.

'It came from over the sea, where it shall never return again,' answered the Princess. And again her eyes began to sparkle with eagerness, and she could scarcely conceal her mirth. 'Lift the cord off my neck and look at it near, and tell me if you ever saw one like it.'

Hildebrandt put out his hands and took hold of the cord, but no sooner were his fingers closed around it than he vanished, and a new bright bead was slung next to the first one on Fiorimonde's chain, and this one was even more beautiful than the other.

The Princess gave a long low laugh, quite terrible to hear.

'Oh, my sweet necklace,' cried she, 'how beautiful you are growing! I think I love you more than anything in the world besides.' Then she went softly back to bed, without anyone hearing her, and fell sound asleep, and slept till Yolande came to tell her it was time for her to get up and dress for the wedding.

The Princess was dressed in gorgeous clothes, and only Yolande noticed that beneath her satin gown, she wore the golden cord, but now there were two beads upon it instead of one. Scarcely was she ready when the King burst into her room in a towering rage.

'My daughter,' cried he, 'there is a plot against us. Lay aside your bridal attire and think no more of Prince Hildebrandt, for he too has disappeared, and is nowhere to be found.'

At this the Princess wept, and entreated that Hildebrandt should be sought for far and near, but she laughed to herself, and said, 'Search where you will, yet you shall not find him'; and so again a great search was made, and when no trace of the Prince was found, all the palace was in an uproar.

The Princess again put off her bride's dress and clad herself in black, and sat alone, and pretended to weep, but Yolande, who watched her, shook her head, and said, 'More will come and go before the wicked Princess has done her worst.'

A month passed, in which Fiorimonde pretended to mourn for Hildebrandt, then she went to the King and said,

'Sire, I pray that you will not let people say that when any bridegroom comes to marry me, as soon as he has seen me he flies rather than be my husband. I beg that suitors may be summoned from far and near that I may not be left alone unwed.'

The King agreed, and envoys were sent all the world over to bid any who would come and be the husband of Princess Fiorimonde. And come they did, kings and princes from south and north, east and west – King Adrian, Prince Sigbert, Prince Algar, and many more – but though all went well till the wedding morning, when it was time to go to church, no bridegroom was to be found. The old King was sadly frightened, and would fain have given up all hope of finding a husband for the Princess, but now she implored him, with tears in her eyes, not to let her be disgraced in this way. And so suitor after suitor continued to come, and now it was known, far and wide, that whoever came to ask for the hand of Princess Fiorimonde vanished, and was seen no more of men. The courtiers were afraid and whispered under their breath, 'It is not right, it cannot be'; but only Yolande noticed how the beads came upon the golden thread, till it was well-nigh covered, yet there always was room for one bead more.

So the years passed, and every year Princess Fiorimonde grew lovelier and lovelier, so that no one who saw her could guess how wicked she was.

In a far off country lived a young prince whose name was Florestan. He had a dear friend named Gervaise, whom he loved better than anyone in the world. Gervaise was tall, and broad, and stout of limb, and he loved Prince Florestan so well, that he would gladly have died to serve him.

It chanced that Prince Florestan saw a portrait of Princess Fiorimonde, and at once swore he would go to her father's court, and beg that he might have her for his wife, and Gervaise in vain tried to dissuade him.

'There is an evil fate about the Princess Fiorimonde,' quoth he; 'many have gone to marry her, but where are they now?'

'I don't know or care,' answered Florestan, 'but this is sure, that I will wed her and return here, and bring my bride with me.'

So he set out for Fiorimonde's home, and Gervaise went with him with a heavy heart.

When they reached the court, the old King received them and

welcomed them warmly, and he said to his courtiers, 'Here is a fine young prince to whom we would gladly see our daughter wed. Let us hope that this time all will be well.' But now Fiorimonde had grown so bold, that she scarcely tried to conceal her mirth.

'I will gladly marry him tomorrow, if he comes to the church,' she said; 'but if he is not there, what can I do?' and she laughed long and merrily, till those who heard her shuddered.

When the Princess's ladies came to tell her that Prince Florestan was arrived, she was in the garden, lying on the marble edge of a fountain, feeding the goldfish who swam in the water.

'Bid him come to me,' she said, 'for I will not go any more in state to meet any suitors, neither will I put on grand attire for them. Let him come and find me as I am, since all find it so easy to come and go.' So her ladies told the prince that Fiorimonde waited for him near the fountain.

She did not rise when he came to where she lay, but his heart bounded with joy, for he had never in his life beheld such a beautiful woman.

She wore a thin soft white dress, which clung to her lithe figure. Her beautiful arms and hands were bare, and she dabbled with them in the water, and played with the fish. Her great blue eyes were sparkling with mirth, and were so beautiful, that no one noticed the wicked look hid in them; and on her neck lay the marvellous many-coloured necklace, which was itself a wonder to behold.

'You have my best greetings, Prince Florestan,' she said. 'And you, too, would be my suitor. Have you thought well of what you would do, since so many princes who have seen me have fled for ever, rather than marry me?' and as she spoke, she raised her white hand from the water, and held it out to the Prince, who stooped and kissed it, and scarcely knew how to answer her for bewilderment at her great loveliness.

Let him come and find me as I am, since all find it easy to come and go

Gervaise followed his master at a short distance, but he was ill at ease, and trembled for fear of what should come.

'Come, bid your friend leave us,' said Fiorimonde, looking at Gervaise, 'and sit beside me, and tell me of your home, and why you wish to marry me, and all pleasant things.'

Florestan begged that Gervaise would leave them for a little, and he walked slowly away, in a very mournful mood.

He went on down the walks, not heeding where he was going, till he met Yolande, who stood beneath a tree laden with rosy apples, picking the fruit, and throwing it into a basket at her feet. He would have passed her in silence, but she stopped him, and said,

'Have you come with the new Prince? Do you love your master?'

'Ay, better than anyone else on the earth,' answered Gervaise. 'Why do you ask?'

'And where is he now?' said Yolande, not heeding Gervaise's question.

'He sits by the fountain with the beautiful Princess,' said Gervaise.

'Then, I hope you have said goodbye to him well, for be assured you shall never see him again,' said Yolande nodding her head.

'Why not, and who are you to talk like this?' asked Gervaise.

'My name is Yolande,' answered she, 'and I am Princess Fiorimonde's maid. Do you not know that Prince Florestan is the eleventh lover who has come to marry her, and one by one they have disappeared, and only I know where they are gone.'

'And where are they gone?' cried Gervaise, 'and why do you not tell the world, and prevent good men being lost like this?'

'Because I fear my mistress,' said Yolande, speaking low and drawing near to him; 'she is a sorceress, and she wears the brave kings and princes who come to woo her, strung upon a cord round her neck. Each one forms the bead of a necklace which she wears, both day and night. I have watched that necklace growing; first it was only an empty gold thread; then came King Pierrot, and when he disappeared the first bead appeared upon it. Then came Hildebrandt, and two beads were on the string instead of one; then followed Adrian, Sigbert, and Algar, and Cenred, and Pharamond, and Baldwyn, and Leofric, and Raoul, and all are gone, and ten beads hang upon the string, and tonight there will be eleven, and the eleventh will be your Prince Florestan.'

'If this be so, cried Gervaise, 'I will never rest till I have plunged my sword into Fiorimonde's heart'; but Yolande shook her head.

'She is a sorceress,' she said, 'and it might be hard to kill her; besides, that might not break the spell, and bring back the princes to life. I wish I could show you the necklace, and you might count the beads, and see if I do not speak the truth, but it is always about her neck, both night and day, so it is impossible.'

'Take me to her room tonight when she is asleep, and let me see it there,' said Gervaise.

'Very well, we will try,' said Yolande; 'but you must be very still, and make no noise, for if she wakes, remember it will be worse for us both.'

When night came and all in the palace were fast asleep, Gervaise and Yolande met in the great hall, and Yolande told him that the Princess slumbered soundly.

'So now let us go,' said she, 'and I will show you the necklace on which Fiorimonde wears her lovers strung like beads, though how she transforms them I know not.'

'Stay one instant, Yolande,' said Gervaise, holding her back, as she would have tripped upstairs. 'Perhaps, try how I may, I shall be beaten, and either die or become a bead like those who have come before me. But if I succeed, and rid the land of your wicked Princess, what will you promise me for a reward?'

'What would you have?' asked Yolande.

'I would have you say you will be my wife, and come back with me to my own land,' said Gervaise.

'That I will promise gladly,' said Yolande, kissing him, 'but we must not speak or think of this till we have cut the cord from Fiorimonde's neck, and all her lovers are set free.'

So they went softly up to the Princess's room, Yolande holding a small lantern, which gave only a dim light. There, in her grand bed, lay Princess Fiorimonde. They could just see her by the lantern's light, and she looked so beautiful that Gervaise began to think Yolande spoke falsely, when she said she was so wicked.

Her face was calm and sweet as a baby's; her hair fell in ruddy waves on the pillow; her rosy lips smiled, and the little dimples showed in her cheeks; her white soft hands were folded amidst the scented lace and linen of which the bed was made. Gervaise almost forgot to look at the glittering beads hung round her throat, in wondering at her loveliness, but Yolande pulled him by the arm.

'Do not look at her,' she whispered softly, 'since her beauty has cost dear already; look rather at what remains of those who thought her as fair as you do now; see here,' and she pointed with her finger to each bead in turn.

'This was Pierrot, and this Hildebrandt, and these are Adrian, and Sigbert, and Algar, and Cenred, and that is Pharamond, and that Raoul, and last of all here is your own master Prince Florestan. Seek him now where you will and you will not find him, and you shall never see him again till the cord is cut and the charm broken.'

'Of what is the cord made?' whispered Gervaise.

'It is of the finest gold,' she answered. 'Nay, do not you touch her lest she wake. I will show it to you.' And Yolande put down the lantern and

Seek him now where you will and you will not find him

softly put out her hands to slip the beads aside, but as she did so, her fingers closed around the golden string, and directly she was gone. Another bead was added to the necklace, and Gervaise was alone with the sleeping Princess. He gazed about him in sore amazement and fear. He dared not call less Fiorimonde should wake.

'Yolande,' he whispered as loud as he dared, 'Yolande where are you?' but no Yolande answered.

Then he bent down over the Princess and gazed at the necklace. Another bead was strung upon it next to the one to which Yolande had pointed as Prince Florestan. Again he counted them. 'Eleven before, now there are twelve. Oh hateful Princess! I know now where go the brave kings and princes who came to woo you, and where, too, is my Yolande,' and as he looked at the last bead, tears filled his eyes. It was brighter and clearer than the others, and of a warm red hue, like the red dress Yolande had worn. The princess turned and laughed in her sleep, and at the sound of her laughter Gervaise was filled with horror and loathing. He crept shuddering from the room, and all night long sat up alone, plotting how he might defeat Fiorimonde, and set Florestan and Yolande free.

Next morning when Fiorimonde dressed she looked at her necklace and counted its beads, but she was much perplexed, for a new bead was added to the string.

'Who can have come and grasped my chain unknown to me?' she said to herself, and she sat and pondered for a long time. At last she broke into weird laughter.

'At any rate, whoever it was, is fitly punished,' quoth she. 'My brave necklace, you can take care of yourself, and if anyone tries to steal you, they will get their reward, and add to my glory. In truth I may sleep in peace, and fear nothing.'

The day passed away and no one missed Yolande. Towards sunset the rain began to pour in torrents, and there was such a terrible thunderstorm that everyone was frightened. The thunder roared, the lightning gleamed flash after flash, every moment it grew fiercer and fiercer. The sky was so dark that, save for the lightning's light, nothing could be seen, but Princess Fiorimonde loved the thunder and lightning.

She sat in a room high up in one of the towers, clad in a black velvet dress, and she watched the lightning from the window, and laughed at each peal of thunder. In the midst of the storm a stranger, wrapped in a cloak, rode to the palace door, and the ladies ran to tell the Princess that a new prince had come to be her suitor. 'And he will not tell his name,' said they, 'but says he hears that all are bidden to ask for the hand of Princess Fiorimonde, and he too would try his good fortune.'

'Let him come at once,' cried the Princess. 'Be he prince or knave what care I? If princes all fly from me it may be better to marry a peasant.'

So they led the newcomer up to the room where Fiorimonde sat. He was wrapped in a thick cloak, but he flung it aside as he came in, and showed how rich was his silken clothing underneath; and so well was he disguised, that Fiorimonde never saw that it was Gervaise, but looked at him, and thought she had never seen him before.

'You are most welcome, stranger prince, who has come through such lightning and thunder to find me,' said she. 'Is it true, then, that you wish to be my suitor? What have you heard of me?'

'It is quite true, Princess,' said Gervaise. 'And I have heard that you are the most beautiful woman in the world.'

'And is that true also?' asked the Princess. 'Look at me now, and see.'

Gervaise looked at her and in his heart he said, 'It is quite true, oh wicked Princess! There never was woman as beautiful as you, and never before did I hate a woman as I hate you now', but aloud he said,

'No, Princess, that is not true; you are very beautiful, but I have seen a woman who is fairer than you for all that your skin looks ivory against your velvet dress, and your hair is like gold.'

'A woman who is fairer than I?' cried Fiorimonde, and her breast began to heave and her eyes to sparkle with rage, for never before had she heard such a thing said. 'Who are you who dares come and tell me of women more beautiful than I am?'

'I am a suitor who asks to be your husband, Princess,' answered Gervaise, 'but still I say I have seen a woman who was fairer than you.'

'Who is she – where is she?' cried Fiorimonde, who could scarcely contain her anger. 'Bring her here at once that I may see if you speak the truth.'

'What will you give me to bring her to you?' said Gervaise. 'Give me that necklace you wear on your neck, and then I will summon her in an instant'; but Fiorimonde shook her head.

'You have asked,' said she, 'for the only thing from which I cannot part,' and then she bade her maids bring her her jewel casket, and she drew out diamonds, and rubies, and pearls, and offered them, all or any, to Gervaise. The lightening shone on them and made them shine and flash, but he shook his head.

'No, none of these will do,' quoth he. 'You can see her for the necklace, but for nothing else.'

'Take it off for yourself then,' cried Fiorimonde, who now was so angry that she only wished to be rid of Gervaise in any way.

'No, indeed,' said Gervaise, 'I am no lady's maid, and should not know how to clasp and unclasp it'; and in spite of all Fiorimonde could say or do, he would not touch either her or the magic chain.

At night the storm grew even fiercer, but it did not trouble the Princess. She waited till all were asleep, and then she opened her bedroom window and chirruped softly to the little brown bird, who flew down from the roof at her call. Then she gave him a handful of peas as before, and he grew and grew and grew till he was as large as an ostrich, and she sat upon his back and flew out through the air, laughing at the lightning and thunder which flashed and roared around her. Away they flew till they came to the old witch's hut, and here they found the witch sitting at her open door catching the lightning to make charms with.

'Welcome, my dear,' croaked she, as Fiorimonde stepped from the bird; 'here is a night we both love well. And how goes the necklace? – right merrily I see. Twelve beads already – but what is that twelfth?' and she looked at it closely.

'Nay, that is one thing I want you to tell me,' said Fiorimonde, drying the rain from her golden hair. 'Last night when I slept there were eleven, and this morning there are twelve; and I know not from whence comes the twelfth.'

'It is no suitor,' said the witch, 'but from some young maid, that that bead is made. But why should you mind? It looks well with the others.'

'Some young maid,' said the Princess. 'Then, it must be Cicely or Marybel, or Yolande, who would have robbed me of my necklace as I slept. But what care I? The silly wench is punished now, and so may all others be, who would do the same.'

'And when will you get the thirteenth bead, and where will he come from?' asked the witch.

'He waits at the palace now,' said Fiorimonde, chuckling. 'And this is why I have to speak to you'; and then she told the witch of the stranger who had come in the storm, and of how he would not touch her necklace, nor take the cord in his hand, and how he said also that he knew a woman fairer than she.

'Beware, Princess, beware,' cried the witch in a warning voice, as she listened. 'Why should you heed tales of other women fairer than you? Have I not made you the most beautiful woman in the world, and can any others do more than I? Give no ear to what this stranger says or you shall rue it.' But still the Princess murmured, and said she did not love to hear anyone speak of others as beautiful as she.

'Be warned in time,' cried the witch, 'or you will have cause to repent it. Are you so silly or so vain as to be troubled because a Prince says idly what you know is not true? I tell you do not listen to him, but let him be slung to your chain as soon as may be, and then he will speak no more.' And then they talked together of how Fiorimonde could make Gervaise grasp the fatal string.

Next morning when the sun rose, Gervaise started off into the woods, and there he plucked acorns and haws, and hips, and strung them on to a string to form a rude necklace. This he hid in his bosom, and then went back to the palace without telling anyone.

When the Princess rose, she dressed herself as beautifully as she could, and braided her golden locks with great care, for this morning she meant her new suitor to meet his fate. After breakfast, she stepped into the garden, where the sun shone brightly, and all looked fresh after the storm. Here from the grass she picked up a golden ball, and began to play with it.

'Go to our new guest,' cried she to her ladies, 'and ask him to come here and play at ball with me.' So they went, and soon they returned bringing Gervaise with them.

'Good morrow, prince,' cried she. 'Pray, come and try your skill at this game with me; and you,' she said to her ladies, 'do not wait to watch our play, but each go your way, and do what pleases you best.' So they all went away, and left her alone with Gervaise.

'Well, prince,' cried she as they began to play, 'what do you think of me by morning light? Yesterday when you came it was so dark, with thunder and clouds, that you could scarcely see my face, but now that there is bright sunshine, pray look well at me, and see if you do not think me as beautiful as any woman on earth,' and she smiled at Gervaise, and looked so lovely as she spoke, that he scarce knew how to answer her; but he remembered Yolande, and said,

'Doubtless you are very beautiful; then why should you mind my telling you that I have seen a woman lovelier than you?'

At this the Princess again began to be angry, but she thought of the witch's words and said,

'Then, if you think there is a woman fairer than I, look at my beads, and now, that you see their colours in the sun, say if you ever saw such jewels before.'

'It is true I have never seen beads like yours, but I have a necklace here, which pleases me better'; and from his pocket he drew the haws and acorns, which he had strung together.

'What is that necklace, and where did you get it? Show it to me!' cried Fiorimonde; but Gervaise held it out of her reach, and said,

'I like my necklace better than yours, Princess; and, believe me, there is no necklace like mine in all the world.'

'Why, is it a fairy necklace? What does it do? Pray give it to me!' cried Fiorimonde, trembling with anger and curiosity, for she thought, 'Perhaps it has power to make the wearer beautiful; perhaps it was worn by the woman whom he thought more beautiful than I, and that is why she looked so fair.'

'Come, I will make a fair exhange,' said Gervaise. 'Give me your necklace and you shall have mine, and when it is round your throat I will truthfully say that you are the fairest woman in the world; but first I must have your necklace.'

'Take it, then,' cried the Princess, who, in her rage and eagerness, forgot all else, and she seized the string of beads to lift it from her neck, but no sooner had she taken it in her hands than they fell with a rattle to the earth, and Fiorimonde herself was nowhere to be seen. Gervaise bent down over the necklace as it lay upon the grass, and, with a smile, counted thirteen beads; and he knew that the thirteenth was the wicked Princess, who had herself met the evil fate she had prepared for so many others.

'Oh, clever Princess!' cried he, laughing aloud, 'you are not so very clever, I think, to be so easily outwitted.' Then he picked up the necklace on the point of the sword and carried it, slung thereon, into the council chamber, where sat the King surrounded by statesmen and courtiers busy with state affairs.

'Pray, King,' said Gervaise, 'send someone to seek for Princess

Fiorimonde. A moment ago she played with me at ball in the garden, and now she is nowhere to be seen.'

The King desired that servants should seek her Royal Highness; but they came back saying she was not to be found.

'Then let me see if I cannot bring her to you; but first let those who have been longer lost than she, come and tell their own tale.' And, so saying, Gervaise let the necklace slip from his sword on to the floor, and taking from his breast a sharp dagger, proceeded to cut the golden thread on which the beads were strung and as he clave it in two there came a mighty noise like a clap of thunder.

'Now'; cried he, 'look, and see King Pierrot who was lost,' and as he spoke he drew from the cord a bead, and King Pierrot, in his royal clothes, with his sword at his side, stood before them.

'Treachery!' he cried, but ere he could say more Gervaise had drawn off another bead, and King Hildebrandt appeared, and after him came Adrian, and Sigbert, and Algar, and Cenred, and Pharamond, and Raoul, and last of the princes, Gervaise's own dear master Florestan, and they all denounced Princess Fiorimonde and her wickedness.

'And now,' cried Gervaise, 'here is she who has helped to save you all,' and he drew off the twelfth bead, and there stood Yolande in her red dress; and when he saw her Gervaise flung away his dagger and took her in his arms, and they wept for joy.

The King and all the courtiers sat pale and trembling, unable to speak for fear and shame. At length the King said with a deep groan.

'We owe you deep amends, O noble kings and princes! What punishment do you wish us to prepare for our most guilty daughter?' but here Gervaise stopped him and said,

'Give her no other punishment than what she has chosen for herself. See, here she is, the thirteenth bead upon the string; let no one dare to draw it off, but let this string be hung up where all people can see it and see the one bead, and know the wicked Princess is punished for her sorcery, so it will be a warning to others who would do like her.'

So they lifted the golden thread with great care and hung it up outside the town hall, and there the one bead glittered and gleamed in the sunlight, and all who saw it knew that it was the wicked Princess Fiorimonde who had justly met her fate.

Then all the kings and princes thanked Gervaise and Yolande, and loaded them with presents, and each went to his own land.

And Gervaise married Yolande, and they went back with Prince Florestan to their home, and all lived happily to the end of their lives.

Two

THE POOL
AND
THE TREE

ONCE THERE WAS A TREE STANDING IN THE MIDDLE OF A VAST wilderness, and beneath the shade of its branches was a little pool, over which they bent. The pool looked up at the tree and the tree looked down at the pool, and the two loved each other better than anything else on earth. And neither of them thought of anything else but each other, or cared who came and went in the world around them.

'But for you and the shade you give me I should have been dried up by the sun long ago,' said the pool.

'And if it were not for you and your shining face, I should never have seen myself, or have known what my boughs and blossoms were like,' answered the tree.

Every year when the leaves and flowers had died away from the branches of the tree, and the cold winter came, the little pool froze over and remained hard and silent till the spring; but directly the sun's rays thawed it, it again sparkled and danced as the wind blew upon it, and it began to watch its beloved friend, to see the buds and leaves reappear, and together they counted the leaves and blossoms as they came forth.

One day there rode over the moorland a couple of travellers in search of rare plants and flowers. At first they did not look at the tree, but as they were hot and tired they got off their horses, and sat under the shade of the boughs, and talked of what they had been doing. 'We have not found much,' said one gloomily; 'it seemed scarcely worth while to come so far for so little.'

'One may hunt for many years before one finds anything very rare,' answered the elder traveller. 'Who knows but we may yet have some luck?' As he spoke he picked up one of the fallen leaves of the tree which lay beside him, and at once he sprang to his feet, and pulled down one of the branches to examine it. Then he called to his comrade to get up, and he also closely examined the leaves and blossoms, and they talked together eagerly, and at length declared that this was the best thing they had found in all their travels. But neither the pool nor the tree heeded them, for the pool lay looking lovingly up to the tree, and the tree gazed down at the clear water of the pool, and they wanted nothing more, and by and by the travellers mounted their horses and rode away.

The summer passed and the cold winds of autumn blew.

'Soon your leaves will drop and you will fall asleep for the winter, and we must bid each other goodbye,' said the pool.

'And you too when the frost comes will be numbed to ice,' answered the tree; 'but never mind, the spring will follow, and the sun will wake us both.'

But long before the winter had set in, ere yet the last leaf had fallen, there came across the prairie a number of men riding on horses and mules, bringing with them a long waggon. They rode straight to the tree, and foremost among them were the two travellers who had been there before.

'Why do they come? What do they want?' cried the pool uneasily;

They wanted nothing more

but the tree feared nothing. The men had spades and pickaxes, and began to dig a deep ditch all round the tree's roots, and then they dug beneath them, and at last both the pool and the tree saw that they were going to dig it up.

'What are you doing? Why are you trying to wrench up my roots and to move me?' cried the tree; 'don't you know that I shall die if you drag me from my pool which has fed and loved me all my life?' And the pool said, 'Oh, what can they want? Why do they take you? The sun will come and dry me up without your shade, and I never, never shall see you again.' But the men heard nothing, and continued to dig at the root of the tree till they had loosened all the earth round it, and then they lifted it and wrapped big cloths round it and put it on their waggon and drove away with it.

Then for the first time the pool looked straight up at the sky without seeing the delicate tracery made by the leaves and twigs against the blue, and it called out to all things near it: 'My tree, my tree, where have they taken my tree? When the hot sun comes it will dry me up, if it shines down on me without the shade of my tree.' And so loudly it mourned and lamented that the birds flying past heard it, and at last

a swallow paused on the wing, and hovering near its surface, asked why it grieved so bitterly. 'They have taken my tree,' cried the pool, 'and I don't know where it is; I cannot move or look to right or left, so I shall never see it again.'

'Ask the moon,' said the swallow. 'The moon sees everywhere, and she will tell you. I am flying away to warmer countries, for the winter will soon be here. Goodbye, poor pool.'

At night, when the moon rose, and the pool looked up and saw its beautiful white face, it remembered the swallow's words, and called out to ask its aid.

'Find me my tree,' it prayed; 'you shone through its branches and know it well, and you can see all over the world; look for my tree, and tell me where they have taken it. Perhaps they have torn it in pieces or burnt it up.'

'Nay,' cried the moon, 'they have done neither, for I saw it a few hours ago when I shone near it. They have taken it many miles away and it is planted in a big garden, but it has not taken root in the earth, and its foliage is fading. The men who took it prize it heartily, and strangers come from far and near to look at it, because they say it is so rare, and there are only one or two like it in the world.'

On hearing this the pool felt itself swell with pride that the tree should be so much admired; but then it cried in anguish, 'And I shall never see it again, for I can never move from here.'

'That is nonsense,' cried a little cloud that was sailing near; 'I was once in the earth like you. Tomorrow, if the sun shines brightly, he will draw you up into the sky, and you can sail along till you find your tree.'

'Is that true?' cried the pool, and all that night it rested in peace waiting for the sun to rise. Next day there were no clouds, and when the pool saw the sun shining it cried, 'Draw me up into the sky, dear Sun, that I may be a little cloud and sail all the world over, till I can find my beloved tree.'

When the sun heard it, he threw down hundreds of tiny golden threads which dropped over the pool, and slowly and gradually it began to change and grow thinner and lighter, and to rise through the air, till at last it had quite left the earth, and where it had lain before, there was nothing but a dry hole, but the pool itself was transformed into a tiny cloud, and was sailing above in the blue sky in the sunshine. There were many other little clouds in the sky, but our little cloud kept apart from them all. It could see far and near over a great space of country, but nowhere could it espy the tree, and again it turned to the sun for help. 'Can you see?' it cried. 'You who see everywhere, where is my tree?'

'You can't see it yet,' answered the sun, 'for it is away on the other side of the world, but presently the wind will begin to blow and it will blow you till you find it.'

Then the wind arose, and the cloud sailed along swiftly, looking everywhere as it went for the tree. It could have had a merry time if it had not longed so for its friend. Everywhere was the golden sunlight shining through the bright blue sky, and the other clouds tumbled and danced in the wind and laughed for joy.

'Why do you not come and dance with us?' they cried; 'why do you sail on so rapidly?'

'I cannot stay, I am seeking a lost friend,' answered the cloud, and it scudded past them, leaving them to roll over and over, and tumble about, and change their shapes, and divide and separate, and play a thousand pranks.

For many hundred miles the wind blew the little cloud, then it said, 'Now I am tired and shall take you no further, but soon the west wind will come and it will take you on; goodbye.' And at once the wind stopped blowing and dropped to rest on the earth; and the cloud stood still in the sky and looked all around.

'I shall never find it,' it sighed. 'It will be dead before I come.'

Presently the sun went down and the moon rose, then the west wind began to blow gently and moved the cloud slowly along.

'Which way should I go, where is it?' entreated the cloud.

'I know; I will take you straight to it,' said the west wind. 'The north wind has told me. I blew by the tree today; it was drooping, but when I told it that you had risen to the sky and were seeking it, it revived and tried to lift its branches. They have planted it in a great garden, and there are railings round it and no one may touch it; and there is one gardener who has nothing to do but to attend to it, and people come from far and near to look at it because it is so rare, and they have only found one or two others like it, but it longs to be back in the desert, stooping over you and seeing its face in your water.'

'Make haste, then,' cried the cloud, 'lest before I reach it I fall to pieces with joy at the thought of seeing it.'

'How foolish you are!' said the wind. 'Why should you give yourself up for a tree? You might dance about in the sky for long yet, and then you might drop into the sea and mix with the waves and rise again with them to the sky, but if you fall about the tree you will go straight into the dark earth, and perhaps you will always remain there, for at the roots of the tree they have made a deep hole and the sun cannot draw you up through the earth under the branches.'

'Then that will be what I long for,' cried the cloud. 'For then I can lie in the dark where no one may see me, but I shall be close to my tree.'

'You are foolish,' said the wind again; 'but you shall have what you want.'

The wind blew the cloud low down near the earth till it found itself over a big garden, in which there were all sorts of trees and shrubs, and such soft green grass as the cloud had never seen before. And there in the middle of the grass, in a bed of earth to itself, with a railing round it so that no one could injure it, was the tree which the cloud had come so far to seek. Its leaves were falling off, its branches were drooping, and its buds dropped before they opened, and the poor tree looked as if it were dying.

'There is my tree, my tree!' called the cloud. 'Blow me down, dear wind, so that I may fall upon it.'

The wind blew the cloud lower and lower, till it almost touched the top branches of the tree. Then it broke and fell in a shower, and crept down through the earth to its roots, and when it felt its drops the tree lifted up its leaves and rejoiced, for it knew that the pool it had loved so had followed it.

'Have you come at last?' it cried. 'Then we need never be parted again.'

In the morning when the gardeners came they found the tree looking quite fresh and well, and its leaves quite green and crisp. 'The cool wind last night revived it,' they said, 'and it looks as if it had rained

too in the night, for round here the earth is quite damp.' But they did not know that under the earth at the tree's roots lay the pool, and that that was what had saved the tree.

And there it lies to this day, hidden away in the darkness where no one can see it, but the tree feels it with its roots, and blooms in splendour, and people come from far and near to admire it.

Three

THE WANDERINGS OF ARASMON

LONG AGO THERE LIVED A WANDERING MUSICIAN AND HIS WIFE, whose names were Arasmon and Chrysea. Arasmon played upon a lute to which Chrysea sang, and their music was so beautiful that people followed them in crowds and gave them as much money as they wanted. When Arasmon played all who heard him were silent from wonder and admiration, but when Chrysea sang they could not refrain from weeping, for her voice was more beautiful than anything they had ever heard before.

Both were young and lovely, and were as happy as the day was long, for they loved each other dearly, and liked wandering about seeing new countries and people and making sweet music. They went to all sorts of places, sometimes to big cities, sometimes to little villages, sometimes to lonely cottages by the seashore, and sometimes they strolled along the green lanes and fields, singing and playing so exquisitely, that the very birds flew down from the trees to listen to them.

One day they crossed a dark line of hills, and came out on a wild moorland country, where they had never been before. On the side of the hill they saw a little village, and at once turned towards it, but as they drew near Chrysea said,

'What gloomy place is this? See how dark and miserable it looks.'

'Let us try to cheer it with some music,' said Arasmon, and began to play upon his lute, while Chrysea sang. One by one the villagers came out of their cottages and gathered round them to listen, but Chrysea thought she had never before seen such forlorn-looking people. They were thin and bent, their faces were pale and haggard, also their clothes looked old and threadbare, and in some places were worn into holes. But they crowded about Arasmon and Chrysea, and begged them to go on playing and singing, and as they listened the women shed tears, and the men hid their faces and were silent. When they stopped, the people began to feel in their pockets as if to find some coins, but Arasmon cried,

'Nay, good friends, keep your money for yourselves. You have not too much of it, to judge by your looks. But let us stay with you for tonight, and give us food and lodging, and we shall think ourselves well paid, and will play and sing to you as much as you like.'

'Stay with us as long as you can, stay with us always,' begged the people; and each one entreated to be allowed to receive the strangers and give them the best they had. So Arasmon and Chrysea played and sang to them till they were tired, and at last, when the heavy rain began to fall, they turned towards the village, but as they passed through its narrow streets they thought the place itself looked even sadder than its inmates. The houses were ill-built, and seemed to be almost tumbling down. The streets were uneven and badly kept. In the gardens they saw no flowers, but dank dark weeds. They went into a cottage which the people pointed out to them, and Arasmon lay down by the fire, calling to Chrysea to rest also, as they had walked far, and she must be weary. He soon fell asleep, but Chrysea sat at the door watching the dark clouds as they drifted over the darker houses. Outside the cottage hung a blackbird in a cage, with drooping wings and scanty plumage. It was the only animal they had yet seen in the village, for of cats or dogs or singing-birds there seemed to be none.

When she saw it, Chrysea turned to the woman of the house, who stood beside her, and said,

'Why don't you let it go? It would be much happier flying about in the sunshine.'

'The sun never shines here,' said the woman sadly. 'It could not pierce through the dark clouds which hang over the village. Besides, we do not think of happiness. It is as much as we can do to live.'

'But tell me,' said Chrysea, 'what is it that makes you so sad and your village such a dreary place? I have been to many towns in my life, but to none which looked like this.'

'Don't you know,' said the woman, 'that this place is spellbound?'

'Spellbound?' cried Chrysea. 'What do you mean?'

The woman turned and pointed towards the moor. 'Over yonder,' she said, 'dwells a terrible old wizard by whom we are bewitched, and he has a number of little dark elves who are his servants, and these are they who make our village what you see it. You don't know how sad it is to live here. The elves steal our eggs, and milk, and poultry, so that there is never enough for us to eat, and we are half-starved. They pull down our houses, and undo our work as fast as we do it. They steal our corn when it is standing in sheaves, so that we find nothing but empty husks'; and as she ceased speaking the woman sighed heavily.

'But if they do all this harm,' said Chrysea, 'why do not some of you go to the moor and drive them away?'

'It is part of the spell,' said the woman, 'that we can neither hear nor see them. I have heard my grandfather say that in the old time this place was no different to others, but one day this terrible old magician came and offered the villagers a great deal of money if they would let him dwell upon the moor; for before that it was covered with golden gorse and heather, and the country folk held all their merrymakings there, but they were tempted with the gold, and sold it, and from that day the elves have tormented us; and as we cannot see them, we cannot get rid of them, but must just bear them as best we may.'

'That is a sad way to speak,' said Chrysea. 'Cannot you find out what the spell really is and break it?'

'It is a song,' said the woman, 'and every night they sing it afresh. It is said that if anyone could go to the moor between midnight and dawn, and could hear them singing it, and then sing through the tune just as they themselves do, the charm would be broken, and we should be free. But it must be someone who has never taken their money, so we cannot do it, for we can neither see nor hear them.'

'But I have not taken their money,' said Chrysea. 'And there is no tune I cannot sing when I have heard it once. So I will go to the moor for you and break the spell.'

'Nay, do not think of such a thing,' cried the woman. 'For the elves are most spiteful, and you don't know what harm they might do to you, even if you set us free.'

Chrysea said no more, but all the evening she thought of what the woman had told her, and still stood looking out into the dismal street. When she went to bed she did not sleep, but lay still till the clock struck one. Then she rose softly, and wrapping herself in a cloak, opened the door and stepped out into the rain. As she passed, she looked up and saw the blackbird crouching in the bottom of its cage. She opened the cage door to let it fly, but still it did not move, so she lifted it out in her hand.

'Poor bird!' said she gently; 'I wish I could give this village its liberty as easily as I can give you yours,' and carrying it with her she walked on towards the moor. It was a large waste piece of land, and looked as though it had been burnt, for the ground was charred and black, and there was no grass or green plant growing on it, but there were some blackened stumps of trees, and to these Chrysea went, and hid herself behind one to wait and see what would come. She watched for a long time without seeing anyone, but at last there rose from the ground not far from her a lurid gleam, which spread and spread until it became a large circle of light, in the midst of which she saw small dark figures moving, like ugly little men. The light was now so bright that she could distinguish each one quite plainly. Never before had she seen anything so ugly, for their faces were twisted and looked cruel and wicked.

They joined hands, and, forming a ring, danced slowly round, and, as they did so, the ground opened, and there rose up in their centre a tiny village exactly like the spellbound village, only that the houses were but a few inches high. Round this the elves danced, and then they began to sing. Chrysea listened eagerly to their singing, and no sooner had they done, than she opened her lips and sang the same tune through from beginning to end just as she had heard it.

Her voice rang out loud and clear, and at the sound the little village crumbled and fell away as though it had been made of dust.

The elves stood silent for a moment, and then with a wild cry they all rushed towards Chrysea, and at their head she saw one about three times the size of the others, who appeared to be their chief.

'Come, quickly, let us punish the woman who has dared to thwart us,' he cried. 'What shall we change her to?'

'A frog to croak on the ground,' cried one.

'No, an owl to hoot in the night,' cried another.

'Oh, for pity's sake,' implored Chrysea, 'don't change me to one of these loathsome creatures, so that, if Arasmon finds me, he will spurn me.'

'Hear her,' cried the chief, 'and let her have her will. Let us change her to no bird or beast, but to a bright golden harp, and thus shall she remain, until upon her strings someone shall play our tune, which she has dared to sing.'

'Agreed!' cried the others, and all began to dance round Chrysea and to sing as they had sung around the village. She shrieked and tried to run, but they stopped her on every side. She cried, 'Arasmon! Arasmon!' but no one came, and when the elves' song was done, and they disappeared, all that was left was a little gold harp hanging upon the boughs of the tree, and only the blackbird who sat above knew what had come of poor Chrysea.

When morning dawned, and the villagers awoke, all felt that some great change had taken place. The heavy cloud which hung above the village had cleared away; the sun shone brightly, and the sky was blue; streams which had been dry for years, were running clear and fresh: and the people all felt strong, and able to work again; the trees were beginning to bud, and in their branches sang birds, whose voices had not been heard there for many a long year. The villagers looked from one to another and said, 'Surely the spell is broken; surely the elves must have fled'; and they wept for joy.

Arasmon woke with the first beam of the sun, and finding Chrysea was not there, he rose, and went to seek her in the village, calling, 'Chrysea, Chrysea! the sun is up and we must journey on our way'; but no Chrysea answered, so he walked down all the streets, calling 'Chrysea! come, Chrysea!' but no Chrysea came. Then he said,

'She has gone into the fields to look for wild flowers, and will soon be back.' So he waited for her patiently, but the sun rose high, the villagers went to their work, and she did not return. At this Arasmon was frightened, and asked everyone he met if they had seen her, but each one shook his head and said, 'No, they had seen nothing of her.'

Then he called some of the men together and told them that his wife had wandered away, and he feared lest she might lose herself and go still farther, and he asked them to help him to look for her. So some went one way, and some another, to search, and Arasmon himself walked for miles the whole country round, calling 'Chrysea! Chrysea!' but no answer came.

The sun was beginning to set and twilight to cover the land, when Arasmon came on to the moor where Chrysea had met her fate. That, too, was changed. Flowers and grass were already beginning to grow there, and the children of the village, who till now had never dared to venture near it, were playing about it. Arasmon could hear their voices as he came near the tree against which Chrysea had leaned, and on which now hung the golden harp. In the branches above sat the blackbird singing, and Arasmon stopped and listened to its song, and thought he had never heard a bird sing so sweetly before. For it sang the magic song by which Chrysea had broken the elves' spell, the first tune it had heard since it regained its liberty.

'Dear blackbird,' said Arasmon, looking up to it, 'I wish your singing could tell me where to find my wife Chrysea'; and as he looked up he saw a golden harp hanging upon the branches, and he took it down and ran his fingers over the strings. Never before did harp give forth such music. It was like a woman's voice, and was most beautiful, but so sad that when Arasmon heard it he felt inclined to cry. It seemed to be calling for help, but he could not understand what it said, though each time he touched the strings it cried, 'Arasmon, Arasmon, I am here! It is I, Chrysea'; but though Arasmon listened, and wondered at its tones, yet he did not know what it said.

He examined it carefully. It was a beautiful little harp, made of pure gold, and at the top was a pair of golden hands and arms clasped together.

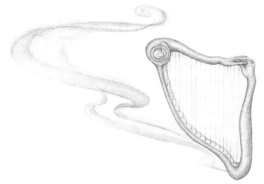

'I will keep it,' said Arasmon, 'for I never yet heard a harp with such a tone, and when Chrysea comes she shall sing to it.'

But Chrysea was nowhere to be found, and at last the villagers declared she must be lost, or herself have gone away on purpose, and that it was vain to seek her farther. At this Arasmon was angry, and saying that he would seek Chrysea as long as he had life, he left the village to wander over the whole world till he should find her. He went on foot, and took with him the golden harp.

He walked for many, many miles far away from the village and the moor, and when he came to any farmhouses, or met any country people on the road he began to play, and everyone thronged round him and stared, in breathless surprise at his beautiful music. When he had done he would ask them, 'Have you seen my wife Chrysea? She is dressed in white and gold, and sings more sweetly than any of the birds of heaven.'

But all shook their heads and said, 'No, she had not been there'; and whenever he came to a strange village, where he had not been before, he called, 'Chrysea, Chrysea, are you here?' but no Chrysea answered, only the harp in his hands cried whenever he touched its strings, 'It is I, Arasmon! It is I, Chrysea!' but though he thought its notes like Chrysea's voice, he never understood them.

He wandered for days and months and years through countries and villages which he had never known before. When night came and he found himself in the fields alone, he would lie down upon his cloak and sleep with his head resting upon the harp, and if by chance one of its golden threads was touched it would cry, 'Arasmon, awake, I am here!' Then he would dream that Chrysea was calling him, and would wake and start up to look for her, thinking she must be close at hand.

One day, towards night, when he had walked far, and was very tired, he came to a little village on a lonely, rocky coast by the sea, and he found that a thick mist had come up, and hung over the village, so that he could barely see the path before him as he walked. But he found his way down to the beach, and there stood a number of fisherwomen, trying to look through the mist towards the sea, and speaking anxiously.

'What is wrong, and for whom are you watching, good folk?' he asked them.

'We are watching for our husbands,' answered one. 'They went out in their boats fishing in the early morning, when it was quite light, and then arose this dreadful fog, and they should have come back long ago, and we fear lest they may lose their way in the darkness and strike on a rock and be drowned.'

'I, too, have lost my wife Chrysea,' cried Arasmon. 'Has she passed by here? She had long golden hair, and her gown was white and gold, and she sang with a voice like an angel's.'

The women all said, 'No, they had not seen her'; but still they strained their eyes towards the sea, and Arasmon also began to watch for the return of the boats.

They waited and waited, but they did not come, and every moment the darkness grew thicker and thicker, so that the women could not see each other's faces, though they stood quite near together.

Then Arasmon took his harp and began to play, and its music floated over the water for miles through the darkness, but the women were weeping so for their husbands, that they did not heed it.

'It is useless to watch,' said one. 'They cannot steer their boats in such a darkness. We shall never see them again.'

'I will wait all night till morning,' said another, 'and all day next day, and next night, till I see some sign of the boats, and know if they be living or dead,' but as she stopped speaking, there rose a cry of 'Here they are,' and two or three fishing-boats were pushed on to the sand close by where they stood, and the women threw their arms round their husbands' necks, and all shouted for joy.

The fishermen asked who it was who had played the harp; 'For,' they said, 'it was that which saved us. We were far from land, and it was so dark that we could not tell whether to go to left or to right, and had no sign to guide us to shore; when of a sudden we heard the most beautiful music, and we followed the sound, and came in quite safely.'

''Twas this good harper who played while we watched,' said the

She sang with a voice like an angel's

women, and one and all turned to Arasmon, and told him with tears of their gratitude, and asked him what they could do for him, or what they could give him in token of their thankfulness; but Arasmon shook his head and said, 'You can do nothing for me, unless you can tell me where to seek my wife Chrysea. It is to find her I am wandering'; and when the women shook their heads, and said again they knew nothing of her, the harp-strings as he touched them cried again.

'Arasmon! Arasmon! listen to me. It is I, Chrysea'; but again no one understood it, and though all pitied him, no one could help him.

Next morning when the mist had cleared away, and the sun was shining, a little ship set sail for foreign countries, and Arasmon begged the captain to take him in it that he might seek Chrysea still farther.

They sailed and sailed, till at last they came to the country for which they were bound; but they found the whole land in confusion, and war and fighting everywhere, and all the people were leaving their homes and hiding themselves in the towns, for fear of a terrible enemy, who was invading them. But no one hurt Arasmon as he wandered on with his harp in his hand, only no one would stop to answer him, when he asked if Chrysea had been there, for everyone was too frightened and hurried to heed him.

At last he came to the chief city where the King dwelt, and here he found all the men building walls and fortresses, and preparing to defend the town, because they knew their enemy was coming to besiege it, but all the soldiers were gloomy and low-spirited.

'It is impossible for us to conquer,' they said, 'for there are three of them to every one of us, and they will take our city and make our King prisoner.'

That night as the watchmen looked over the walls, they saw in the distance an immense army marching towards them, and their swords and helmets glittered in the moonlight.

Then they gave the signal, and the captains gathered together their men to prepare them for fighting; but so sure were they of being beaten that it was with difficulty their officers could bring them to the walls.

'It would be better,' said the soldiers, 'to lay down our arms at once and let the enemy enter, for then we should not lose our lives as well as our city and our wealth.'

When Arasmon heard this he sat upon the walls of the town, and began to play upon his harp, and this time its music was so loud and clear, that it could be heard far and wide, and its sound so exultant and joyous, that when the soldiers heard it they raised their heads, and their fears vanished, and they started forward, shouting and calling that they would conquer or be killed.

Then the enemy attacked the city, but the soldiers within met them with so much force that they were driven back, and had to fly, and the victorious army followed them and drove them quite out of their country, and Arasmon went with them, playing on his harp, to cheer them as they went.

When they knew the victory was theirs, all the captains wondered what had caused their sudden success, and one of the lieutenants said, 'It was that strange harper who went with us, playing on his harp. When our men heard it they became as brave as lions.' So the captains sent for Arasmon, but when he came they were astonished to see how worn and thin he looked, and could scarcely believe it was he who had made such wonderful music, for his face had grown thin and pale, and there were grey locks in his hair.

They asked him what he would like to have, saying they would give him whatever he would choose, for the great service he had done them.

Arasmon only shook his head and said,

'There is nothing I want that you can give me. I am seeking the whole world round to find my wife Chrysea. It is many many years since I lost her. We two were as happy as birds on the bough. We wandered over the world singing and playing in the sunshine. But now she is gone, and I care for nothing else.' And the captains looked pityingly at him, for they all thought him mad, and could not understand what the harp said when he played on it again, and it cried,

'Listen, Arasmon! I too am here – I, Chrysea.'

So Arasmon left that city, and started again, and wandered for days and months and years.

He came by many strange places, and met with many strange people, but he found no trace of Chrysea, and each day he looked older and sadder and thinner.

At length he came to a country where the King loved nothing on earth so much as music. So fond of it was he, that he had musicians and singers by the score, always living in his palace, and there was no way of pleasing him so well as by sending a new musician or singer. So when Arasmon came into the country, and the people heard how marvellously he played, they said at once, 'Let us take him to the King. The poor man is mad. Hear how he goes on asking for his wife; but, mad or not, his playing will delight the King. Let us take him at once to the palace.' So, though Arasmon would have resisted them, they dragged him away to the court, and sent a messenger to the King, to say they had found a poor mad wandering harper, who played music the like of which they had never heard before.

The King and Queen, and all the court, sat feasting when the messenger came in saying that the people were bringing a new harper to play before his majesty.

'A new harper!' quoth he. 'That is good hearing. Let him be brought here to play to us at once.'

So Arasmon was led into the hall, and up to the golden thrones on which sat the King and Queen. A wonderful hall it was, made of gold and silver, and crystal and ivory, and the courtiers, dressed in blue and green and gold and diamonds, were a sight to see. Behind the throne were twelve young maids dressed in pure white, who sang most sweetly, and behind them were the musicians who accompanied them on every kind of instrument. Arasmon had never in his life seen such a splendid sight.

'Come here,' cried the King to him, 'and let us hear you play.' And the singers ceased singing, and the musicians smiled scornfully, for they could not believe Arasmon's music could equal theirs. For he looked to be in a most sorry plight. He had walked far, and the dust of the roads was on him. His clothes were worn threadbare, and stained and soiled, while his face was so thin and anxious and sad that it was pitiful to see; but his harp of pure shining gold was undulled, and untarnished. He began to play, and then all smiles ceased, and the women began to weep, and the men sat and stared at him in astonishment. When he had done the King started up, and throwing his arms about his neck, cried, 'Stay with me. You shall be my chief musician. Never before have I heard playing like yours, and whatever you want I will give you.' But when he heard this, Arasmon knelt on one knee and said,

'My gracious lord, I cannot stay. I have lost my wife Chrysea. I must search all over the world till I find her. Ah! how beautiful she was, and how sweetly she sang; her singing was far sweeter than even the music of my harp.'

'Indeed!' cried the King. 'Then I too would fain hear her. But stay with me, and I will send messengers all over the world to seek her far and near, and they will find her much sooner than you.'

So Arasmon stayed at the court, but he said that if Chrysea did not come soon he must go farther to seek her himself.

The King gave orders that he should be clad in the costliest clothes and have all he could want given to him, and after this he would hear no music but Arasmon's playing, so all the other musicians were jealous, and wished he had never come to the palace. But the strangest thing was that no one but Arasmon could play upon his golden harp. All the King's harpers tried, and the King himself tried also, but when they touched the strings there came from them a strange, melancholy wailing, and no one but Arasmon could bring out its beautiful notes.

But the courtiers and musicians grew more and more angry with Arasmon, till at last they hated him bitterly, and only wanted to do him some harm; for they said,

'Who is he, that our King should love and honour him before us? After all, it is not his playing which is so beautiful; it is chiefly the harp on which he plays, and if that were taken from him he would be no better than the rest of us'; and then they began to consult together as to how they should steal his harp.

One hot summer evening Arasmon went into the palace gardens, and sat down to rest beneath a large beech tree, when a little way off he saw two courtiers talking together, and heard that they spoke of him, though they did not see him or know he was there.

'The poor man is mad,' said one; 'of that there is little doubt, but, mad or not, as long as he plays on his harp the King will not listen to anyone else.'

'The only way is to take the harp from him,' said the other. 'But it is hard to know how to get it away, for he will never let it go out of his hands.'

'We must take it from him when he is sleeping,' said the first.

'Certainly,' said the other; and then Arasmon heard them settle how and when they would go to his room at night to steal his harp.

He sat still till they were gone, and then he rose, and grasping the harp tenderly, turned from the palace and walked away through the garden gates.

'I have lost Chrysea,' he said, 'and now they would take from me even my harp, the only thing I have to love in all this world, but I will go away, far off where they will never find me,' and when he was out of sight, he ran with all his might, and never rested till he was far away on a lonely hill, with no one near to see him.

The stars were beginning to shine though it was not yet dark. Arasmon sat on a stone and looked at the country far and near. He could hear the sheep bells tinkling around him, and far, far off in the distance he could see the city and the palace he had left.

Then he began to play on his harp, and as he played the sheep stopped browsing and drew near to listen.

The stars grew brighter and the evening darker, and he saw a woman carrying a child coming up the hill.

She looked pale and tired, but her face was very happy as she sat down not far from Arasmon and listened to his playing, whilst she looked eagerly across the hill as if she watched for someone who was coming. Presently she turned and said, 'How beautifully you play; I never heard music like it before, but what makes you look so sad? Are you unhappy?'

'Yes,' said Arasmon, 'I am very miserable. I lost my wife Chrysea many years ago, and now I don't know where she can be.'

'It is a year since I have seen my husband,' said the woman. 'He went to the war a year ago, but now there is peace and he is coming back, and tonight he will come over this hill. It was just here we parted, and now I am come to meet him.'

'How happy you must be,' said Arasmon. 'I shall never see Chrysea again,' and as he spoke he struck a chord on the harp, which cried, 'O Arasmon, my husband! why do you not know me? It is I, Chrysea.'

'Do not say that,' continued the woman; 'you will find her some day. Why do you sit here? Was it here you parted from her?'

Then Arasmon told her how they had gone to a strange desolate village and rested there for the night, and in the morning Chrysea was gone, and that he had wandered all over the world looking for her ever since.

'I think you are foolish,' said the woman; 'perhaps your wife has been waiting for you at that village all this time. I would go back to the place where I parted from her if I were you, and wait there till she returns. How could I meet my husband if I did not come to the spot where we last were together? We might both wander on for ever and never find each other; and now, see, here he is coming,' and she gave a cry of joy and ran to meet a soldier who was walking up the hill.

Arasmon watched them as they met and kissed, and saw the father lift the child in his arms, then the three walked over the hill together, and when they were gone he sat down and wept bitterly. 'What was it she said?' he said. 'That I ought to go back to the spot where we parted. She will not be there, but I will go and die at the place where I last saw her.' So again he grasped his harp and started. He travelled many days and weeks by land and sea, till late one day he came in sight of the hill on which stood the little village. But at first he could not believe that he had come to the right place, so changed did all appear. He stopped and looked around him in astonishment. He stood in a shady lane, the arching trees met over his head. The banks were full of spring flowers, and either side of the hedge were fields full of young green corn.

'Can this be the wretched bare road down which we walked together? I would indeed it were, and that she were with me now,' said he. When he looked across to the village, the change seemed greater still. There were many more cottages, and they were trim and well kept, standing in neat gardens full of flowers. He heard the cheerful voices of the peasants and the laughter of the village children. The whole place seemed to be full of life and happiness. He stopped again upon the mound where he and Chrysea had first played and sung.

'It is many, many a long year since I was here,' he said. 'Time has changed all things strangely; but it would be hard to say which is the more altered, this village or I, for then it was sunk in poverty and wretchedness, and now it has gained happiness and wealth, and I, who was so happy and glad, now am broken-down and worn. I have lost my only wealth, my wife Chrysea. It was just here she stood and sang, and now I shall never see her again or hear her singing.'

There came past him a young girl driving some cows, and he turned and spoke to her. 'Tell me, I beg,' he said, 'is not your village much changed of late years? I was here long ago, but I cannot now think it the same place, for this is as bright and flourishing a town as I have ever seen, and I remember it only as a dreary tumble-down village where the grass never grew.'

'Oh!' said the girl, 'then you were here in our bad time, but we do not now like to speak of that, for fear our troubles should return. Folks say we were spellbound. 'Tis so long ago that I can scarcely remember it, for I was quite a little child then. But a wandering musician and his wife set us free; at least, everything began to mend after they came, and now we think they must have been angels from heaven, for next day they went, and we have never seen them since.'

'It was I and my wife Chrysea,' cried Arasmon. 'Have you seen her? Has she been here? I have sought all over the world ever since, but I cannot find her, and now I fear lest she be dead.'

The girl stared at him in surprise. 'You? you poor old man. Of what are you talking? You must surely be mad to say such things. These musicians were the most beautiful people upon the earth, and they were young and dressed in shining white and gold, and you are old and grey and ragged, and surely you are very ill too, for you seem to be so weak that you can scarcely walk. Come home with me, and I will give you food and rest till you are better.'

Arasmon shook his head. 'I am seeking Chrysea,' he said, 'and I will rest no more till I have found her'; and the girl, seeing that he was determined, left him alone and went on her way driving her cows before her.

When she had gone Arasmon sat by the wayside and wept as though his heart would break. 'It is too true,' he said; 'I am so old and worn that when I find her she will not know me,' and as he again fell a-weeping his hand struck the harpstrings, and they cried, 'I have watched you through all these years, my Arasmon. Take comfort, I am very near,' and his tears ceased, and he was soothed by the voice of the harp, though he knew not why.

Then he rose. 'I will go to the moor,' he said, 'and look for the tree on which I found my harp, and that will be my last resting place, for surely my strength will carry me no farther.' So he tottered slowly on, calling, as he went, in a weak voice, 'Chrysea, my Chrysea! are you here? I have sought you over the world since you left me, and now that I am old and like to die, I am come to seek you where we parted.'

When he came upon the moor, he wondered again at the change of all the country round. He thought of the charred, blackened waste on which he had stood before, and now he looked with amazement at the golden gorse, the purple heather, so thick that he could scarcely pick his way amongst it.

'It is a beautiful place now,' he said, 'but I liked it better years ago, deserted and desolate though it was, for my Chrysea was here.'

There were so many trees upon the common that he could not tell which was the one on which his harp had hung, but, unable to go any farther, he staggered and sank down beneath a large oak tree, in whose branches a blackbird was singing most sweetly. The sun was setting just as of yore when he had found his harp, and most of the birds' songs were over, but this one bird still sang sweet and clear, and Arasmon, tired and weak though he was, raised his head and listened.

'I never heard bird sing like that,' he said. 'What is the tune it sings? I will play it on my harp before I die.' And with what strength remained to him he reached forth his trembling hand, and grasping his harp struck upon it the notes of the bird's song, then he fell back exhausted, and his eyes closed.

At once the harp slid from his hand, and Chrysea stood beside him – Chrysea dressed as of old, in shining white and gold, with bright hair and eyes.

'Arasmon!' she cried, 'see, it is I, Chrysea!' but Arasmon did not move. Then she raised her voice and sang more sweetly than the bird overhead, and Arasmon opened his eyes and looked at her.

'Chrysea!' cried he; 'I have found my wife Chrysea!' and he laid his head on her bosom and died. And when Chrysea saw it her heart broke, and she lay beside him and died without a word.

In the morning when some of the villagers crossed the common they saw Arasmon and Chrysea lying beneath the oak tree in each other's

He searched everywhere for her

arms, and drew near them, thinking they were asleep, but when they saw their faces they knew they were dead.

Then an old man stooped and looked at Chrysea, and said,

'Surely it is the woman who came to us and sang long ago, when we were in our troubles; and, though he is sadly changed and worn, it is like her husband who played for her singing.'

Then came the girl who had driven the cows and told them how she had met Arasmon, and all he had said to her.

'He searched everywhere for his wife, he said,' said she. 'I am glad he has found her. Where could she be?'

'Would that we had known it was he,' said they all, 'how we would have greeted him! but see, he looks quite content and as if he wished nothing more, since he has found his wife Chrysea.'

Four

THE STORY OF A CAT

ONCE THERE LIVED AN OLD GENTLEMAN WHO WAS A VERY rich old gentleman, and able to buy nearly everything he wanted. He had earned all his wealth for himself by trading in a big city, and now he had grown so fond of money that he loved it better than anything else in the world, and thought of nothing except how he could save it up and make more. But he never seemed to have time to enjoy himself with all that he had earned, and he was very angry if he was asked to give money to others. He lived in a handsome house all alone, and he had a very good cook who cooked him a sumptuous dinner every day, but he rarely asked anyone to share it with him, though he loved eating and drinking, and always had the best of wine and food. His cook and his other servants knew that he was greedy and hard, and cared for nobody, and though they served him well because he paid them, they none of them loved him.

It was one Christmas, and the snow lay thick upon the ground, and the wind howled so fiercely that the old gentleman was very glad he was not obliged to go out into the street, but could sit in his comfortable armchair by the fire and keep warm.

'It really is terrible weather,' he said to himself, 'terrible weather'; and he went to the window and looked out into the street, where all the pavements were inches deep in snow. 'I am very glad that I need not go out at all, but can sit here and keep warm for today, that is the great thing, and I shall have some ado to keep out the cold even here with the fire.'

He was leaving the window, when there came up in the street outside an old man, whose clothes hung in rags about him, and who looked half frozen. He was about the same age as the old gentleman inside the window, and the same height, and had grey, curly hair, like his, and if they had been dressed alike anyone would have taken them for two brothers.

'Oh, really,' said the old gentleman irritably, 'this is most annoying. The parish ought to take up these sort of people, and prevent their wandering about the streets and molesting honest folk,' for the poor old man had taken off his hat, and began to beg.

'It is Christmas Day,' he said, and though he did not speak very loud, the old gentleman could hear every word he said quite plainly through the window. 'It is Christmas Day, and you will have your dinner here in your warm room. Of your charity give me a silver shilling that I may go into an eating-shop, and have a dinner too.'

'A silver shilling!' cried the old gentleman, 'I never heard of such a thing! Monstrous! Go away, I never give to beggars, and you must have done something very wicked to become so poor.'

But still the old man stood there, though the snow was falling on his shoulders, and on his bare head. 'Then give me a copper,' he said; 'just one penny, that today I may not starve.'

'Certainly not,' cried the old gentleman; 'I tell you I never give to beggars at all.' But the old man did not move.

'Then,' he said, 'give me some of the broken victuals from your table, that I may creep into a doorway and eat a Christmas dinner there.'

'I will give you nothing,' cried the old gentleman, stamping his foot.

'Go away. Go away at once, or I shall send for the policeman to take you away.'

The old beggar man put on his hat and turned quietly away, but what the old gentleman thought was very odd was, that instead of seeming distressed he was laughing merrily, and then he looked back at the window, and called out some words, but they were in a foreign tongue, and the old gentleman could not understand them. So he returned to his comfortable armchair by the fire, still murmuring angrily that beggars ought not to be allowed to be in the streets.

Next morning the snow fell more thickly than ever, and the streets were almost impassable, but it did not trouble the old gentleman, for he knew he need not go out and get wet or cold. But in the morning when he came down to breakfast, to his great surprise there was a cat on the hearthrug in front of the fire, looking into it, and blinking lazily. Now the old gentleman had never had any animal in his house before, and he at once went to it and said 'Shoo-shoo!' and tried to turn it out. But the cat did not move, and when the old gentleman looked at it nearer, he could not help admiring it very much. It was a very large cat, grey and black, and had extremely long soft hair, and a thick soft ruff round its neck. Moreover, it looked very well fed and cared for, and as if it had always lived in comfortable places. Somehow it seemed to the old gentleman to suit the room and the rug and the fire, and to make the whole place look more prosperous and cosy even than it had done before.

'A fine creature! a very handsome cat!' he said to himself; 'I should really think that a reward would be offered for such an animal, as it has evidently been well looked after and fed, so it would be a pity to turn it away in a hurry.'

One thing struck him as very funny about the cat, and that was that though the ground was deep in snow and slush outside, the cat was quite dry, and its fur looked as if it had just been combed and brushed. The old gentleman called to his cook and asked if she knew how the cat had come in, but she declared she had not seen it before, and said she believed it must have come down the chimney as all the doors and windows had been shut and bolted. However, there it was, and when his own breakfast was finished the old gentleman gave it a large saucer of milk, which it lapped up not greedily or in a hurry, but as if it were quite used to good food and had had plenty of it always.

'It really is a very handsome animal, and most uncommon,' said the old gentleman, 'I shall keep it awhile and look out for the reward'; but though he looked at all the notices in the street and in the newspapers, the old gentleman could see no notice about a reward being offered for a grey and black cat, so it stayed on with him from day to day.

Every day the cat seemed to his master to grow handsomer and handsomer. The old gentleman never loved anything but himself, but he began to take a sort of interest in the strange cat, and to wonder what sort it was – if it was a Persian or a Siamese, or some curious new sort of which he had never heard. He liked the sound of its lazy contented purring after its food, which seemed to speak of nothing but comfort and affluence. So the cat remained on till nearly a year had passed away.

It was not very long before Christmas that an acquaintance of the old gentleman's came to his rooms on business. He knew a great deal about all sorts of animals and loved them for their own sakes, but of course he had never talked to the old gentleman about them, because he knew he did not love anything. But when he saw the grey cat, he said at once –

'Do you know that this is a very valuable creature, and I should think would be worth a great deal?'

At these words the old gentleman's heart beat high. Here, he thought, would be a piece of great luck if a stray cat could make him richer than he was before.

'Why, who would want to buy it? he said. 'I don't know anybody who would be so foolish as to give any money for a cat which is of no use in life except to catch mice, when you can so easily get one for nothing.'

'Ah, but many people are very fond of cats, and would give much for rare sorts like this. If you want to sell it, the right thing would be to send it to the Cat Show, and there you would most likely take a prize for it, and then someone would be sure to buy it, and, it may be, would give a great deal. I don't know what kind it is, or where it comes from, for I have never seen one the least like it, but for that reason it is very sure to be valuable.'

Upon this the old gentleman almost laughed with joy.

'Where is the Cat Show?' he asked; 'and when is it to be held?'

'There will be a Cat Show in this city quite soon,' said his acquaintance; 'and it will be a particularly good one, for the new Princess is quite crazy about cats, and she is coming to it, and it is said that she doesn't mind what she gives for a cat if she sees one she likes.'

So then he told the old gentleman how he should send his name and the cat's name to the people who managed the show, and where it was to be held, and went away, leaving the old gentleman well pleased, but to himself he laughed and said, 'I don't think that old man thinks of anything on earth but making money. How pleased he was at the idea of selling that beautiful cat if he could get something for it!'

When he had gone, the grey puss came and rubbed itself about its master's legs, and looked up in his face as though it had understood the conversation, and did not like the idea of being sent to the show. But the old gentleman was delighted, and sat by the fire and mused on what he was likely to get for the cat, and wondered if it would not take a prize.

'I shall be sorry to have to send it away,' he said; 'still, if I could get a good round sum of money it would be a real sin not to take it, so you will have to go, puss; and it really was extraordinary good luck for me that you ever came here.'

The days passed, and Christmas Day came, and again the snow fell, and the ground was white. The wind whistled and blew, and on Christmas morning the old gentleman stood and looked out of the window at the falling snow and rain, and the grey cat stood beside him, and rubbed itself against his hand. He rather liked stroking it, it was so soft and comfortable, and when he touched the long hair he always thought of how much money he should get for it.

This morning he saw no old beggar man outside the window, and he said to himself: 'I really think they manage better with the beggars than they used to, and are clearing them from the town.'

But just as he was leaving the window he heard something scratching outside, and there crawled on to the windowsill another cat. It was a very different creature to the grey cat on the rug. It was a poor, thin, wretched-looking animal, with ribs sticking through its fur, and it mewed in the most pathetic manner, and beat itself against the pane. When it saw it, the handsome grey puss was very much excited, and ran to and fro, and purred loudly.

'Oh, you disgraceful-looking beast!' said the old gentleman angrily;

'go away, this is not the place for an animal like you. There is nothing here for stray cats. And you look as if you had not eaten anything for months. How different to my puss here!' and he tapped against the window to drive it away. But still it would not go, and the old gentleman felt very indignant, for the sound of its mewing was terrible. So he opened the window, and though he did not like to touch the miserable animal, he took it up and hurled it away into the snow, and it trotted away, and in the deep snow he could not see the way it went.

But that evening, after he had had his Christmas dinner, as he sat by the fire with the grey puss on the hearthrug beside him, he heard again the noise outside the window, and then he heard the stray cat crying and mewing to be let in, and again the grey and black cat became very much excited, and dashed about the room, and jumped at the window as if it wanted to open it.

'I shall really be quite glad when I have sold you at the Cat Show,' said the old gentleman, 'if I am going to have all sorts of stray cats worrying here,' and for the second time he opened the window, and seized the trembling, half-starved creature, and this time he threw it with all his might as hard as he could throw. 'And now there is an end of you, I hope,' he said as he heard it fall with a dull thud, and settled himself again in his armchair, and the grey puss returned to the hearthrug, but it did not purr or rub itself against its master.

Next morning when he came down to breakfast, the old gentleman poured out a saucer of milk for his cat as usual. 'You must be well fed if you are going to be shown at the show,' he said, 'and I must not mind a little extra expense to make you look well. It will all be paid back, so this morning you shall have some fish as well as your milk.' Then he put the saucer of milk down by the cat, but it never touched it, but sat and looked at the fire with its tail curled round it.

'Oh, well, if you have had so much already that you don't want it, you can take it when you do,' so he went away to his work and left the saucer of milk by the fire. But when he came back in the evening, there was the saucer of milk and the piece of fish, and the grey cat had not touched them. 'This is rather odd,' said the old gentleman; 'however, I suppose cook has been feeding you.'

Next morning it was just the same. When he poured out the milk the cat wouldn't lap it, but sat and looked at the fire. The old gentleman felt a little anxious, for he fancied that the animal's fur did not look so bright as usual, and when in the evening and the next day and the next, it would not lap its milk, or even smell the nice pieces of fish he gave it, he was really uncomfortable. 'The creature is getting ill,' he said, 'and this is most provoking. What will be the use of my having kept it for a year, if now I cannot show it?' He scolded his cook for having given it unwholesome food, but the cook swore it had had nothing. Anyhow it was growing terribly thin, and all day long sat in front of the fire with its tail hanging down, not curled up neatly round it, and its coat looked dull and began to come out in big tufts of hair.

'Now really I shall have to do something,' said the old gentleman, 'it is enough to make anyone angry! No one would believe that this could be a prize cat. It looks almost as wretched as that stray beast that came to the window on Christmas Day.' So he went to a cat and dog doctor, who lived near, and asked him to come in and see a very beautiful cat which had nothing the matter with it, but which refused to eat its food. The cat's doctor came and looked at the cat, and then looked very grave, and shook his head, and looked at it again.

'I don't know what sort of cat it is,' he said ; 'for I never saw any other like it, but it is a very handsome beast, and must be very valuable. Well, I will leave you some medicine for it, and I hope you may be able to pull it round, but with these foreign cats you never know what ails them, and they are hard to cure.'

Now the day was close at hand when the cat should have been sent to the show, and the old gentleman was getting more and more uneasy, for the grey cat lay upon the rug all day and never moved, and its ribs could almost be seen through its side, so thin had it grown. And oddly enough the old gentleman, who had never cared for anyone or anything in his life except himself, began to feel very unhappy, not only because of not getting the money, but because he did not like to think of losing the cat itself. He sent for his friend who had first told him about the Cat Show, and asked his advice, but his friend could not tell him what to do with it.

'Well, well,' he said, 'this is a bad business, for I have told everyone that you are going to exhibit a most extraordinarily beautiful cat, and now this poor creature is really fit for nothing but the knacker's yard. I think, maybe, some naturalist would give you a good price for its skin, as it is so very uncommon, and if I were you I should kill it at once, for if it dies a natural death its skin won't be worth a brass farthing.' At these words the grey cat lifted its head, and looked straight into the old gentleman's face, as if it could understand, and for the first time for many a long year, the old gentleman felt a feeling of pity in his heart, and was angry with his friend for his suggestion.

'I won't have it killed,' he cried; 'why, I declare, though it does seem absurd, I have lived with this creature for a year, and I feel as if it were my friend, and if it would only get well and sit up on the hearthrug, I shouldn't mind about the money one bit!'

At this his friend was greatly astonished, and went away wondering, while the old gentleman sat by the fire and watched the cat lying panting on the rug.

'Poor pussy, poor old pussy!' he said, 'it is a pity that you can't speak and tell me what you want. I am sure I would give it to you.' Just as he spoke there came a noise outside, and he heard a mewing, and looking through the window he saw the same thin ugly brown cat that had come there last Christmas, and it looked as thin and wretched as ever. When she heard the sound the grey cat stood up on her tottering feet and tried to walk to the window. This time the old gentleman did not drive it away, but looked at it, and almost felt sorry for it; it looked almost as thin and ill as his own grey puss.

'You are an ugly brute,' he said, 'and I don't want you always hanging about; still, maybe you would be none the worse for a little milk now, and it might make you look better.' So he opened the window a little, and then he shut it and then he opened it again, and this time the brown cat crawled into the room, and went straight to the hearthrug to the grey puss. There was a big saucer of milk on the hearthrug, and the brown cat began to lap it at once, and the old gentleman never stopped it.

He thought as he watched it, that it grew fatter under his eyes as it drank, and when the saucer was empty he took a jug and gave it some more. 'I really am an old fool,' he said; 'that is a whole penny's worth of milk.' No sooner had he poured out the fresh milk than the grey cat raised itself, and sitting down by the saucer began to lap it as well, as if it were quite well. The old gentleman stared with surprise. 'Well, this is the queerest thing,' he said. So he took some fish and gave it to the strange cat, and then, when he offered some to his own puss, it ate it as if there was nothing the matter. 'This is most remarkable,' said the old gentleman; 'perhaps it was the company of a creature of its own sort that my cat needed, after all.' And the grey cat purred and began to rub itself against his legs.

So for the next few days the two cats lay together on the hearthrug,

Perhaps, 'twas a fairy cat

and though it was too late to send the grey cat to the show, the old gentleman never thought about it, so pleased was he that it had got well again.

But seven nights after the stray cat had come in from outside, as the old gentleman lay asleep in bed at night, he felt something rub itself against his face, and heard his cat purring softly, as though it wanted to say 'goodbye.' 'Be quiet, puss, and lie still till the morning,' he said. But when he came down to have his breakfast in the morning, there sat the brown tabby, looking fat and comfortable by the fire, but the grey cat was not there, and though they looked for it everywhere, no one could find it, though all the windows and doors had been shut, so they could not think how it could have got away. The old gentleman was very unhappy about it, but he looked at the strange cat on his hearth and said, 'it would be unkind now to send this poor thing away, so it may as well stay here.'

When she heard him speaking of its being unkind, his old cook burst out laughing. 'Perhaps,' she said, ''twas a fairy cat, as it could get away through bolts and locks, and nothing but a fairy could have taught my master to think of a thing being unkind or not. I only hope that now he'll think of someone in this world besides himself and his money.' And

sure enough from that time the old gentleman began to forget about his money, and to care for the people about him, and it was all the doing of the strange cat who had come from no one knew where, and gone away to no one knew where.

THE
RAIN
MAIDEN

ONCE UPON A TIME THERE LIVED A SHEPHERD AND HIS WIFE, who lived in a very lonely little cottage far from town or village, near some mountains. It was a wild neighbourhood, and the wind blew across the mountains fiercely, and the rain often fell so heavily that it seemed as if the cottage would be washed away. One evening when the shepherd was out, there came on a great storm of rain which beat against the doors and the windows violently. As the shepherd's wife sat listening to it by the fire, it seemed to her as if it sounded louder than she had ever heard it before, and the raindrops sounded like the knock of a hand that was knocking to gain admittance. It went on for a little time, till the shepherd's wife could bear to listen to it no longer, and she rose and went to the door to open it, though she knew that she would let the wind and rain into the room. As she opened the door a gust of rain was blown in her face, and then she saw that in the doorway stood a woman who had been knocking. She was a tall woman wrapped in a grey cloak with long hair falling down her back. 'Thank you,' she said. And though her voice was very low, the shepherd's wife could hear it plainly through all the storm. 'Thank you for opening the door to me. Many would have let me stand outside. Now may I come into your cottage and rest?'

'How wet you must be!' cried the shepherd's wife; 'come in and rest, and let me give you food. Have you come from far?'

'No, I come from quite near,' said the woman, and she came into the cottage as she spoke, and sat down in a chair near the door. 'And I want not food, only a glass of water. I must go on directly, but I have not far to go, and I shall be no wetter than I am now.'

The shepherd's wife stared in surprise, for she saw that apparently the woman's clothes were not wet at all. And what was stranger still, though she had thought she was only clad in a dull grey cloak, now she saw that she was covered with jewellery – clear stones, like diamonds with many flashing colours; and she also saw that all her clothes were of the finest. She gave her a glass of water, and begged that as well she might give her other food, but the woman shook her head, and said no, water was all she needed. When she had drunk the water she gave back the glass to the shepherd's wife, and said, 'And so this is your home. Have you all that you want in life? Are you happy?'

'Ay, we are happy enough,' said the shepherd's wife, 'save indeed for one thing. Ten years ago my little baby girl died, and I have no other children. I long for one sorely, that I might take care of it and make it happy, while it is little, and then in turn, when I am old, it would love and care for me.'

'And if you had a little child,' said the woman, rising up and standing before the shepherd's wife, 'you think you would really love it better than anything in the world. Many women say that, but few do it. Before long a little child will be born to you, and as long as you love it better than anything in the world it will remain with you, but when you love anything else better than your little daughter and her happiness, it will go from you; so remember my words. Goodbye,' and the woman walked to the door and went quietly out into the rain, and the shepherd's wife

saw her disappearing, and the rain pelting around her, but her clothes were not blown about, neither did the rain seem to wet her.

A year passed away, and the shepherd's wife had a tiny daughter, a lovely little baby with the bluest eyes and the softest skin; the evening she was born the wind howled and the rain fell as fiercely as on the night when the grey woman had come into the shepherd's cottage. The shepherd and his wife both loved their little daughter very dearly, as well they might, as no fairer child was ever seen. But as she grew older, some things about her frightened her mother, and she had some ways of which she could not cure her. She would never go near a fire, however cold she was, neither did she love the sunshine, but always ran from it and crept into the shade; but when she heard the rain pattering against the windowpanes she would cry, 'Listen, mother, listen to my brothers and sisters dancing,' and then she would begin to dance too in the cottage, her little feet pattering upon the boards; or, if she possibly could, she would run out on to the moor and dance, with the rain falling upon her, and her mother had much ado to get her to come back into the cottage, yet she never seemed to get very wet, nor did she catch cold. A river ran near the cottage, and by it she would go and sit for hours dabbling her feet in the water, and singing sweet little songs to herself. Still, in all other ways she was a good, affectionate girl, and did all that her mother told her, and seemed to love both her parents tenderly, and the shepherd's wife would say to herself, 'My only trouble is that when she is grown up, she will want to marry, and leave me, and I shall have to do without her.' Time passed, and the old shepherd died, but his wife and daughter still lived on in the little cottage, and the daughter grew to be a most beautiful young maiden. Her eyes were clear light blue, like the colour of the far-off sea, but it was difficult to say what was the colour of her hair, save that it was very light, and hung in heavy masses over her brow and shoulders. Once or twice her mother felt sorely frightened about her; it was when spring showers were falling, and the young girl had gone into the little garden in front of the cottage to let the rain fall upon her head and face, as she loved to do, in spite of all her mother could say. Then she began to dance, as she always did when the rain fell, and as she danced the sun came out while the rain was yet falling. Her mother watched her from the cottage window, but while she watched her it seemed to her as if her daughter was covered with jewels of every colour, clear and bright; they hung around her in chains, and made her look more like a king's daughter than a shepherd's girl. 'Come in, child, come in,' called the shepherd's wife, and when the young girl came in the cottage all traces of the jewels had gone, and when her mother upbraided her for going out to dance in the rain, she only answered, 'It hurts no one, my mother, and it pleases me, why should you stop me?'

A little way from the cottage on the mountain side stood an old castle, where formerly the Kings of the land used to come and stay, but which now had not been used for very many years. One day, however, the shepherd's wife saw great preparations were being made to beautify and adorn it, and she knew that the King and his son were coming to stay there again. Soon after they had arrived, the shepherd's daughter went down to the river, as was her wont, and sat on the bank, dipping her feet in the ripples. Presently there came up a boat, and it was a grand young man dressed all in velvet and gold who leaned over the side to fish.

'Who are you, and what are you doing here?' cried the shepherd's daughter, for she was afraid of no one.

'I am the King's son,' said he, 'and I am coming here to fish. Who are you, and where do you come from, for I have never seen such a beautiful maiden in my life?' and he looked at her and could scarce speak, so beautiful did she seem to him.

'It is cruel to take the fishes out of the water,' cried the shepherd's daughter, 'leave them alone, and come and dance on the bank with me,' and she went under the shade of a large tree, and began to dance, and the King's son watched her, and again he thought so beautiful a maid there had never been.

Day after day he came down to the river to fish, and day after day he left the line and tackle to sit and watch the shepherd's daughter, and each time found her more enchanting. Once he tried to kiss her hand, but she sprang from him and left him sitting in his boat alone. At last a day came when the Prince said to his father, 'My father, you want me to wed so that I may have an heir to the throne, but there is only one woman that can ever be my wife, and that is the daughter of the poor woman who lives in the little cottage out yonder.'

At first the old King was very wroth, but he loved his son well, and knew that nothing would shake him from his word, so he told him that if he would bring home his bride, he too would rejoice and love her as his daughter even though she be a beggar maid. Then the young Prince rode down to the cottage, and went in and told the shepherd's wife how he had seen her daughter, and loved her and wished to make her his wife,

Come and dance with me

so that she would be Queen of the country.

The shepherd's wife went nearly wild with joy. 'To think that my daughter should be the Queen,' she said to herself, and when her daughter came into the cottage she did not know how to contain herself, but folded her in her arms and kissed her, crying and declaring that never was woman so blessed.

'What has happened, my mother? and what has pleased you so?' said her daughter, while still the shepherd's wife rejoiced and wept for joy.

'It is the King's son, my girl, the King's own son, and he has just been here, and he loves you because you are so beautiful, and he will marry you and make you Queen of all the land. Was there ever such luck for a poor woman?'

But the daughter only said, 'But I don't want to marry the King's son, mother, or anyone. I will never be the wife of any man; I will stay with you and nurse you when you are old and sick, for I can live in no house but this cottage, and have no friend but my mother.'

On hearing this the shepherd's wife became very angry, and told her daughter that she must be mad, and that she must wait for a day or two, and she would be only too thankful for the love of the King's son, and for the honour he was going to do her in making her his Queen. But still the daughter shook her head, and said quite quietly, 'I will never be the wife of the King's son.' The shepherd's wife did not dare tell the King's son what her daughter had said, but told him that he had better speak to her himself if he wished to make her his wife. Then when he was again sitting in the boat on the river, and the maiden on the bank, the King's son told her how much he loved her, and that he would share with her all that he had in this world. But the shepherd's daughter only shook her head and said, 'I will never live at the palace, and I will never be a Queen.'

The old King had ordered great preparations to be made for the wedding, which was to take place immediately, and all sorts of fine clothes were ordered for the shepherd's daughter, that she might appear properly as the wife of the Prince, but for the few days just before the wedding, the rain fell as it had never been known to have fallen; it beat through the roofs of the cottages, and the river swelled and overflowed its banks; everyone was frightened, save indeed the shepherd's daughter, who went out into the wet and danced as was her wont, letting the torrents fall upon her head and shoulders.

But the evening before the wedding day she knelt beside her mother's side. 'Dear mother,' she said, 'let me stop with you and nurse you when you are old. Do not send me away to the palace to live with the King's son.'

Then the mother was very angry, and told her daughter that she was very ungrateful, and she ought to be thankful that such luck had come in her way, and who was she, the daughter of a poor shepherd, that she should object to marrying the King's son?

All night long the rain fell in torrents, and when next day the shepherd's daughter was dressed in all her finery, it was through pools on the ground that she had to step into the grand carriage which the King had sent to fetch her, and while the marriage-service was being read, the priest's voice could scarcely be heard for the pattering of the drops upon the roof, and when they went into the castle to the banquet, the water burst through the doors opened to receive them, so that the King and the wedding guests had hard ado to keep dry. It was a grand feast, and the King's son sat at one end of the table, and his young wife was beside him dressed in white and gold. All the courtiers and all the fine guests declared that surely the world had never contained such a beautiful young women as their future Queen. But just when the goblets were filled with wine, to drink to the health of the bride and bridegroom, there came a cry, 'The floods! the floods!' and the servants ran into the hall, crying out that the waters were pouring in, and in one moment the rooms were filled with water, and no one thought of anything but to save themselves. When the hurricane had subsided, and the waters gone down, they looked around for the Prince's wife, who was nowhere to be found. Everyone said that she had been swept away by the torrents, and that she had been drowned in all her youth and beauty; only the shepherd's wife wept alone, and remembered the words of the woman who came to her on the night of the storm: 'When you love aught on earth better than your daughter and her happiness, she will go from you.'

The King's son mourned his wife, and for long would not be comforted; but when many years had passed, he married a beautiful Princess, and with her lived very happily; only when the rain fell in torrents and beat against the windowpanes it would seem to him as if he heard the sound of dancing feet, and a voice that called out, 'Come and dance with me, come and dance with me and my brothers and sisters, oh King's son, and feel our drops upon your face.'

Six

THE STORY OF THE OPAL

THE SUN WAS SHINING BRIGHTLY ONE HOT SUMMER DAY, AND A little Sunbeam slid down his long golden ladder, and crept unperceived under the leaves of a large tree. All the Sunbeams are in reality tiny Sun-fairies, who run down to earth on golden ladders, which look to mortals like the rays of the Sun. When they see a cloud coming they climb their ladders in an instant, and draw them up after them into the Sun.

The Sun is ruled by a mighty fairy, who every morning tells his tiny servants, the beams, where they are to shine, and every evening counts them on their return, to see he has the right number. It is not known, but the Sun and Moon are enemies, and that is why they never shine at the same time. The fairy of the Moon is a woman, and all her beams are tiny women, who come down on the loveliest little ladders, like threads of silver. No one knows why the Sun and Moon quarrelled. Once they were very good friends. Some say it is because the Sun wished to marry her, and she did not want to, but preferred a sea king, for whose sake she always keeps near the world. Others think it is because of a piece of land which the Moon claimed as her own, and on which the Sun one day shone so strongly that he dried up and killed all the plants and grass there, which offended the Moon very much. Anyhow, it remains that they are bitter enemies, and the Sunbeams and Moonbeams may not play together.

On the day on which my story begins, the Sunbeam about which I am going to tell you crept into a tree, and sat down near a Bullfinch's nest, and watched the Bullfinch and its mate.

'Why should I not have a mate also?' he said to himself; and then he began to feel very sad, for the Sunbeams never mate. Yet he was the prettiest little fellow you could imagine. His hair was bright gold, and he sat still, leaning one arm on his tiny ladder, and listening to the chatter of the birds.

'But I shall try to keep awake tonight to see her,' said a young Bullfinch.

'Nonsense!' said its mother. 'You shall do no such thing.'

'But the Nightingale says she is so very lovely,' said a Wren, looking out from her little nest in a hedge close by.

'The Nightingale!' said the old Bullfinch, scornfully. 'Everyone knows that the Nightingale was moonstruck long ago. Who can trust a word he says?'

'Nevertheless, I should like to see her,' said the Wren.

'I have seen her, and the Nightingale is right,' said a Wood-dove in its soft, cooing tones. 'I was awake last night and saw her; she is more lovely than anything that ever came here before.'

'Of whom were you talking?' asked the Sunbeam; and he shot across to the Bullfinch's nest. All the birds were silent when they saw him. At last the Bullfinch said, 'Only of a Moonbeam, your Highness. No one your Highness would care about,' for the Bullfinch remembered the quarrel between the Sun and Moon, and did not like to say much.

'What is she like?' asked the Sunbeam. 'I have never seen a Moonbeam.'

'I have seen her, and she is as beautiful as an angel,' said the Wood-dove. 'But you should ask the Nightingale. He knows more about her than anyone, for he comes out to sing to her.'

'Where is the Nightingale?' asked the Sunbeam.

'He is resting now,' said the Wren, 'and will not say a word. But later, as the Sun begins to set, he will come out and tell you.'

'At the time when all the decent birds are going to roost,' grumbled the Bullfinch.

'I will wait till the Nightingale comes,' said the Sunbeam.

So all day long he shone about the tree. As the Sun moved slowly down, his ladder dropped with it lower and lower, for it was fastened to the Sun at one end; and if he had allowed the Sun to disappear before he had run back and drawn it up, the ladder would have broken against the earth, and the poor little Sunbeam could never have gone home again, but would have wandered about, becoming paler and paler every minute, till at last he died.

But some time before the Sun had gone, when it was still shining in a glorious bed of red and gold, the Nightingale arose, and, coming forth from his concealment, began to sing loud and clear.

'Oh, is it you at last?' said the Sunbeam. 'How I have waited for you! Tell me about this Moonbeam of whom they are all talking.'

'What shall I tell you of her?' sang the Nightingale. 'She is more beautiful than the rose. She is the most beautiful thing I have ever seen. Her hair is silver, and the light of her eyes is far more lovely than yours. But why should you want to know about her? You belong to the Sun, and hate Moonbeams.'

'I do not hate them,' said the Sunbeam sadly. 'What are they like? Show this one to me some night, dear Nightingale.'

'I cannot show her to you now,' answered the Nightingale; 'for she will not come out till long after the Sun has set; but wait a few days, and when the Moon is full she will come a little before the Sun sets, and if you hide beneath a leaf you may look at her. But you must promise not to shine on her, or you might hurt her, or break her ladder.'

'I will promise,' said the Sunbeam, and every day he came back to the same tree at sunset, to talk to the Nightingale about the Moonbeam, till the Bullfinch was quite angry.

'Tonight I shall see her at last,' he said to himself, for the Moon was almost full, and would rise before the Sun had set. He hid in the oak leaves, trembling with expectation.

'She is coming!' said the Nightingale, and the Sunbeam peeped out from the branches, and watched. In a minute ot two a tiny silver ladder like a thread was placed among the leaves, near the Nightingale's nest, and down it came the Moonbeam, and our little Sunbeam looked out and saw her.

She did not at all look like he had expected she would, but he agreed with the Nightingale that she was the loveliest thing he had ever seen. She was all silver, and pale greeny blue. Her hair and eyes shone like stars. All the Sunbeams looked bright, and hot, but she looked as cool as the sea; yet she glittered like a diamond. The Sunbeam gazed at her in surprise, unable to say a word, till all at once he saw that his little ladder was bending. The Sun was sinking, and he had only just time to scramble back, and draw his ladder after him.

The Moonbeam only saw his light vanishing, and did not see him.

'To whom were you talking, dear Nightingale?' she asked, putting her beautiful white arms around his neck, and leaning her head on his bosom.

'To a Sunbeam,' answered the Nightingale. 'Ah, how beautiful he is! I was telling him about you. He longs to see you.'

'I have never seen a Sunbeam,' said the Moonbeam, wistfully. 'I should like to see one so much'; and all night long she sat close by the Nightingale, with her head leaning on his breast whilst he sang to her of the Sunbeam; and his song was so loud and clear that it awoke the Bullfinch, who flew into a rage, and declared that if it went on any longer she would speak to the Owl about it, and have it stopped. For the Owl was chief judge, and always ate the little birds when they did not behave themselves.

But the Nightingale never ceased, and the Moonbeam listened till the tears rose in her eyes and her lips quivered.

'Tonight, then, I shall see him,' whispered the Moonbeam, as she kissed the nightingale and bid him adieu.

'And tonight he will see you,' said the Nightingale, as he settled to rest among the leaves.

All the next day was cloudy, and the Sun did not shine, but towards evening the clouds passed away and the Sun came forth, and no sooner had it appeared than the Nightingale saw our Sunbeam's ladder placed close to his nest, and in an instant the Sunbeam was beside him.

'Dear, dear nightingale,' he said caressingly, 'you are right. She is more lovely than the dawn. I have thought of her all night and all day. Tell me, will she come again tonight? I will wait to see her.'

'Yes, she will come, and you may speak to her, but you must not touch her,' said the Nightingale; and then they were silent and waited.

Underneath the oak tree lay a large white Stone, a common white Stone, neither beautiful nor useful, for it lay there where it had fallen, and bitterly lamented that it had no object in life. It never spoke to the birds, who scarcely knew it could speak; but sometimes, if the Nightingale lighted upon it, and touched it with his soft breast, or the Moonbeam shone upon it, it felt as if it would break with grief that it should be so stupid and useless. It watched the Sunbeams and Moonbeams come down on their ladders, and wondered that none of the birds but the Nightingale thought the Moonbeam beautiful. That evening, as the Sunbeam sat waiting, the Stone watched it eagerly, and when the Moonbeam placed her tiny ladder among the leaves, and slid down it, it listened to all that was said.

At first the Moonbeam did not speak, for she did not see the Sunbeam, but she came close to the Nightingale, and kissed him as usual.

'Have you seen him again?' she asked. And on hearing this, the Sunbeam shot out from among the green leaves, and stood before her.

For a few minutes she was silent; then she began to shiver and sob, and drew nearer to the Nightingale, and if the Sunbeam tried to approach her, she climbed up her ladder, and went farther still.

'Do not be frightened, dearest Moonbeam,' cried he piteously; 'I would not, indeed, do you any harm, you are so very lovely, and I love you so much.'

The Moonbeam turned away sobbing.

'I do not want you to love me,' she said, 'for if you touch me I shall die. It would have been much better for you not to have seen me; and now I cannot go back and be happy in the Moon, for I shall be always thinking of you.'

'Could it have been better not to love, as I love you? I do not care if I die or not, now that I have seen you; and see,' said the Sunbeam sadly, 'my end is for sure, for the Sun is fast sinking, and I shall not return to it, I shall stay with you.'

'Go, while you have time,' cried the Moonbeam. But even as she spoke the Sun sank beneath the horizon, and the tiny gold ladder of the Sunbeam broke with a snap, and the two sides fell to earth and melted away.

'See,' said the Sunbeam, 'I cannot return now, neither do I wish it. I will remain here with you till I die.'

'No, no,' cried the Moonbeam. 'Oh, I shall have killed you! What shall I do? And look, there are clouds drifting near the Moon; if one of them floats across my ladder it will break it. But I cannot go and leave you here'; and she leaned across the leaves to where the Sunbeam sat, and looked into his eyes. But the Nightingale saw that a tiny white cloud was sailing close by the Moon – a little cloud no bigger than a spot of white wool, but quite big and strong enough to break the Moonbeam's little ladder.

'Go, go at once. See! your ladder will break,' he sang to her; but she did not notice him, but sat watching the Sunbeam sadly. For a moment

the Moon's light was obscured, as the tiny cloud sailed past it; then the little silver ladder fell to earth, broken in two and shrunk away; but the Moonbeam did not heed it.

'It does not matter,' she said, 'for I should never have gone back and left you here, now that I have seen you.'

So all night long they sat together in the oak tree, and the Nightingale sang to them, and the other birds grumbled that he kept them awake. But the two were very happy, though the Sunbeam knew he was growing paler every moment, for he could not live twenty-four hours away from the Sun.

When the dawn began to appear, the Moonbeam shivered and trembled.

'The strong Sun,' she said, 'would kill me, but I fear something even worse than the Sun. See how heavy the clouds are! Surely it is going to rain, and rain would kill us both at once. Oh, where can we look for shelter before it comes?'

The Sunbeam looked up, and saw that the rain was coming.

'Come,' he said, 'let us go'; and they wandered out into the forest, and sought for a sheltering place, but every moment they grew weaker.

When they were gone, the Stone looked up at the Nightingale, and said:

'Oh, why did they go? I like to hear them talk, and they are so pretty; they can find no shelter out there, and they will die at once. See! in my side there is a large hole where it is quite dark, and into which no rain can come. Fly after them and tell them to come; that I will shelter them.' So the Nightingale spread his wings, and flew singing:

'Come back, come back! The Stone will shelter you. Come back at once before the rain falls.'

They had wandered out into an open field, but when she heard the

Every night he sings their story and that is why his song is so sad

Nightingale, the Moonbeam turned her head and said:

'Surely that is the Nightingale singing. See! he is calling us.'

'Follow me,' sang the bird. 'Back at once to shelter in the Stone.' But the Moonbeam tottered and fell.

'I am grown so weak and pale,' she said, 'I can no longer move.'

Then the Nightingale flew to earth. 'Climb upon my back,' he said, 'and I will take you both back to the Stone.' So they both sat upon his back, and he flew with them to the large Stone beneath the tree.

'Go in,' he said, stopping in front of the hole; and both passed into the hole, and nestled in the darkness within the Stone.

Then the rain began. All day long it rained, and the Nightingale sat in his nest half asleep. But when the Moon rose, after the Sun had set, the clouds cleared away, and the air was again full of tiny silver ladders, down which the Moonbeams came, but the Nightingale looked in vain for his own particular Moonbeam. He knew she could not shine on him again, therefore he mourned, and sang a sorrowful song. Then he flew down to the Stone, and sang a song at the mouth of the hole, but there came no answer. So he looked down the hole, into the Stone, but there was no trace of the Sunbeam or the Moonbeam – only one shining spot of light, where they had rested. Then the Nightingale knew that they had faded away and died.

'They could not live away from the Sun and Moon,' he said. 'Still, I wish I had never told the Sunbeam of her beauty; then she would be here now.' So all night long he sang his saddest songs, and told their story again and again.

When the Bullfinch heard of it she was quite pleased. 'Now, at last,' she said, 'we shall hear the end of the Moonbeam. I am heartily glad, for I was sick of her.'

'How much they must have loved each other!' said the Dove. 'I am glad at least that they died together,' and she cooed sadly.

But through the Stone wherein the beams had sheltered, shot up bright beautiful rays of light, silver and gold. They coloured it all over with every colour of the rainbow, and when the Sun or Moon warmed it with their light it became quite brilliant. So that the Stone, from being the ugliest thing in the whole forest, became the most beautiful.

Men found it and called it the Opal. But the Nightingale knew that it was the Sunbeam and Moonbeam who, in dying, had suffused the Stone with their mingled colours and light; and the Nightingale will never forget them, for every night he sings their story, and that is why his song is so sad.

'Fairy country is a moon-and-star charmed land'

MARY DE MORGAN